KU-728-249

Brian Stableford
Swan Song

Pan Books London and Sydney

First published in Great Britain 1978 by Pan Books Ltd,
Cavaye Place, London SW10 9PG
© Brian M. Stableford 1975
ISBN 0 330 25400 6
Printed and bound in Great Britain by
Hunt Barnard Printing Ltd, Aylesbury, Bucks

Swan Song

Born in 1948 at Shipley in Yorkshire, Brian Stableford claims to be undistinguished apart from being a brilliant poker player, an expert at word games and having webbed toes. He is self-educated, but was processed by Manchester Grammar School and the University of York where he took a first class degree in biology. He also qualified for a B. Phil. in sociology at York. He taught sociology at Reading in 1976 and re-joined the department as a lecturer in 1977.

He has written numerous SF novels – notably the *Hooded Swan* series which are published as Pan paperbacks. He has also written a book of popularized science – *The Mysteries of Modern Science* and is currently working on a historical sociology of witchcraft and demonology, taken over from the late James Blish.

Previously published by
Brian Stableford in Pan Books

Dedication
for Ceri

Chasing freedom can be a very tiring game. It's the sort of game that dominates your thought and endeavor for months or years—endurance isn't a problem as long as you have some kind of effort to make and some kind of direction to go—and then, when you win it, you're left utterly and absolutely flat. Empty and exhausted. Drained of all purpose, impetus, and ambition. The first taste of hard-won freedom is inevitably as foul as stagnant water. It can be the first time in your life that you can't find an answer to the question *why,* and when you've been fighting *that* hard for *that* long, the lack of such an answer can be frightening.

It only takes time to get back into yourself, but that time can hang so limp and useless it makes you sweat to wear it.

In the end, it's OK. It's worth the feeling absolutely flat, let down like a worn-out balloon, provided that you can know the only way is up and you're all set to start climbing. It's not the bottom of the spiritual well or the ladder back up to the good air which really threatens you . . . it's the past you left so recently behind, the past that's sitting on your footprints, the past which can always run after you, can always catch you up, if it can only think of a motive. . . .

. . . A reason to drag you back down.

When the *Sandman* touched down on Erica I was in no hurry to leap out of her and get dirt between my toes. There was nothing about honest soil which appealed to me at that particular point in time. There were one or two little things in my province which needed sorting, and I was happy enough to sort, although two hours any time in the next two days would set everything up, and I was bound to be asked to do a tour of duty as officer-of-the-watch.

After a while, though, I began to get bored. I wandered down to the engine room to see if I could catch Sam Parks before he ducked ship and ran for the big city lights. I had a lot of things I wanted to complain about, and he wouldn't take offense if I bitched at him. Also, of course, he might be able to drop me a hint as to how to get the complaints heard somewhere that mattered. I had a suspicion that a lot of valuable breath could go to waste without my getting the slightest satisfaction from the noble captain.

Sam was still cleaning up in the engine room, if "cleaning up" is the right expression to describe turning a disaster into a mess.

"Does it bitch itself up like that every trip?" I asked, in sympathetic tones.

"Hello, Grainger," he said. "I already know." He looked up at me with his gray eyes, which had retreated somewhat with advancing age until they were almost in the shadow of his fading eyebrows, except when he looked up. He straightened briefly, easing a kink in his back. He was a big man—or had been—but he was as thin as a rake. His hands looked too big for his slender wrists, as though they'd been stuck on as an ironic afterthought. Sam was a giant designed by a committee who wanted to go easy on materials.

'What do you know already?" I asked.

"Everything you're going to tell me. It's all true and there isn't a damn thing I can do about it."

"Nobody's blaming you," I said.

"Doesn't matter who blames who," he said, sounding totally resigned. "Things is what they seem. A mess. Same down here, as you can see. I reckon I'd be prepared to ride a decent drive-unit into hell, just for the pleasure of its company."

"You could get a better ship than this," I said, meaning a nice clean passenger job, though I wasn't about to say so in case he was a proud man and took offense.

He shook his head. "Too old," he said. "Couldn't pass the medical. What's your excuse?"

"I was in a hurry," I said. "What does the captain think of his wonderful ship?"

"The captain doesn't think. He only waits. Promotion is slow but loyalty pays its miserable dividends eventually. The faster we fall to pieces the happier he'll be. He ain't going places but he's got years under his hat yet. Go see him if you want to. He'll be half expecting you. He'll give you the old story—and it's true, so you can't argue. He can't afford it, whatever it is. He can't afford to get a downship crew in to attend to what we have, let alone replace any of it. He *can't* afford it—God's truth. It's not his ship. He has his margins, same as anyone else. Anyone thinks the margins are too narrow on the *Sandman,* they jack it in. That's how come you're employed; but don't be grateful."

"I thought your last pilot might have died of shame," I said, trying to inject a little wit into the downbeat tone of the conversation.

"He was no good," said Sam. "Of all the parts needed replacing he was number one on the list."

"So OK," I said. "He's replaced. Be happy."

He shrugged away the note of irony in my voice. I tried to shrug it away as well. I'd picked up the *Sandman* on Ludlock. It was by no means the sort of operation I wanted to stay with, but it was too close to the core for berths to be easy to come by. I needed to be farther out into the inner ring before I could begin to make real plans. The *Sandman* would get me there eventually, if I managed to hold her together without too much sealing wax in her seams. It's a hard life, but it goes on.

I still had most of the cash that remained to me once I'd bought myself free of all obligations to Titus Charlot and the shadows which trailed him, but it wasn't all that much of a stake and it wouldn't carry me far into the civilized galaxy or into the future. Ideally I wanted to buy myself a slice of a ship, but with inflation the way it was courtesy of the Caradoc/Star Cross stranglehold on interplanetary commerce the chance was becoming more remote by the hour. I had to live on whatever was offered and a purseful of hope. The *Sandman* had been on offer.

She was a squat, untidy d-skipper, built cheap somewhere on the Solar wing. She handled in a manner that was faintly reminiscent of the old *Fire-Eater* that Lapthorn and I had used to trundle away our youth, and felt privileged so to do. The *Sandman* wasn't quite as old as the *Fire-Eater*, but she was by no means this year's model, or even last year's. It wasn't that she was horribly dangerous or difficult to fly—but she was damned uncomfortable and capable of giving sixty percent efficiency at the best. She was slow, cumbersome, and a real pig's bastard in atmosphere. On takeoff she acted like a bronchial case with a hangover and she landed like a drunk coming down a ladder. Apart from that she was home, for the time being.

"Couldn't we do her up a bit between ourselves?" I asked.

Sam had returned to his slow and unmethodical tidying-up while I'd been thinking quietly to myself. Now he looked up again with a distant expression on his face. I realized that his complexion had once been as pale as his eyes, before the radiation tan got to his skin and polished it up like dark wood. For a second or two, his eyes failed to focus, and I knew there was more than one reason why he'd fail a medical if he were forced to take one. He'd spent his life looking at a lot of hot light. I wondered how old he was, in real years. Maybe the same age as me. He could probably live to see fifty-five, if he retired now to chew grass on some dirtside haven where the labor problem was nine parts solved. Otherwise . . .

After a pause, he said, "We might. If we had the time and the inclination. Pigs might also fly. No pay, no thanks, and a flogged-out gut is what we'd end up with. You volunteer?"

His voice held a hint of bitter sarcasm. He was getting at me, just a little. He knew I'd been running ships that made this one look like scrap metal, and he knew I'd owned my own in the past. He couldn't help resenting it, just a little. It occurred to me that he really would love pouring a bucketful of sweat into a ship like the *Hooded Swan*, if that could be anything more than a dream. But this wasn't my ship or his, not in the real sense. We were here to stay alive and get paid. Sure, we could ginger up the baby—but for nothing, or less than nothing. We'd probably lose out on pay because if she could go faster she could work faster and there'd be less pay for space time.

"Suppose I were to request politely that the contacts

could be trimmed?" I said. "It's no fun hooking up to
that column. It feels like I'm being garotted."

Sam shrugged. It was none of his business. But the way
his eyes dropped told me that there wasn't much chance.

I accepted the situation without grace, but without
much bitterness. In all likelihood I would have to go at
the captain anyhow, if I got the chance. I would complain long and hard. But it would only be for the good of
his soul and mine.

"It's a living," said Sam. He didn't sound as if he meant
it—much.

"Any idea where we're liable to be going in the near
future?" I asked him.

"Nowhere," he said. "Lots of it." He waved a hand
indicatively. 'Hop, skip, and hop again. No jump, not for
a while. Wait for some luck. That captain's one hell of a
smartass when it comes to cheating dirtsquatters. In time,
he'll land us a little role. Then we go somewhere decent
for a while. The company doesn't need to ask too many
questions. Anyone's entitled to a look at the living now
and again."

I nodded. It was no more than I expected. No ship working this kind of territory was going to be taking long hauls
unless she had effort in hand. Her margins were too narrow. She'd hop a handful of light-years at a time, picking
up crumbs and swapping marbles. It might be months before we touched somewhere important enough to warrant
my hanging around waiting for something to turn up—
somewhere that opportunity might call once now and
again to give a quick knock. Perhaps I could have made
it to the inner ring faster by taking one ship at a time
and keeping my direction out from the heart stars, but
that would be risky. I might get stranded and I'd certainly get poorer. Far better to stick with the *Sandman*
and be patient. If it took six months, six months it took.
You can't command the future from where I was.

"You've been around these parts all your life?" I
asked him, to manufacture conversation.

"I know my way around," he said. He looked at me
and he grinned.

"I used to work the outer rim," I said. "Mostly."

'Never could stand wide-open spaces," he said.

The hatch behind me was open, and somebody on

their way out of the belly of the ship paused to look in on us. It was a kid whose name I didn't know. Chief bottle-washer and cargo-humper, and part-time everything as the occasion demanded. The captain generally called him "Hey you," or—not so often—"What the hell are you doin'?" Everyone else probably did the same. It's easy to lose or gain names out in space.

"You got seckin watch, Turpin," he said, with an odd flattening accent that I'd not heard before. "Better mik most of the evenin'." He paused as he glanced sideways at me. "You're OK," he said, deliberately avoiding any direct manner of address. "Free till timorrow."

"Thanks," said Sam. I nodded acknowledgment.

"Captain still aboard?" I asked. I knew the other spare crewman had already gone. He'd been in the cockpit with me when we touched and he'd gone out like a rabbit. Apparently, he had urgent business of one kind or another on the ground.

"Naw," said the engineer, waving the kid away. "He'll be in his cabin, but not *in*, if you see what I mean. He'll crawl around the port as soon as the jumboes have cleared the cargo—he won't be fit to talk to till tomorrow, when he'll have his mind on a lift again. He shouldn't have to beg for cargo—the port knew we were on regular run, and they got a standing arrangement to fix us up. Unless the big company's expanding its operation to cut us out."

"What company's that?" I asked.

He looked at me a little sharply. "Zacher's lot," he said. "The something-or-other lifting company. Something like that."

"Never heard of it," I said.

"You could have signed on with 'em where we picked you up, if you'd wanted to," he said. He thought I was already sick to death of the *Sandman*.

I shook my head. "Don't like the big men and the sign-on," I said.

He looked away again. He knew the score. He probably valued his own soul too much to put it in hock.

I turned away to go back to the cockpit, but he interrupted me. "I'm going out in a couple of minutes," he said. "If you want to come with me. I know my way around. Here and everywhere."

I didn't hesitate. "Okay," I said.

"Don't bother the captain," he said. "Just lock your cabin door."

"Sure," I said.

I waited for him outside. I looked around the field at all the rust-buckets sitting on the tarpol. There were six, but one of them just *had* to be a derelict. I couldn't imagine that anybody intended to lift it. Of the others, two were obviously based here—transports owned by communities or planet-based operations which had found something to dig up and ship out to somewhere else in the vicinity, just to keep the micro-economy ticking over. The others were operative ships, cleaner and tougher, but not new. I assumed that one, at least, must belong to the company Sam had talked about. Even a relatively small company with a name like the something-or-other lifting company could probably keep a couple of hundred ships on a rim-to-rim shuttle covering a two-fifty-world circuit and clean up pretty comprehensively. Come the time when the *Sandman* and all the other small-time operators like her got run clear out of the black edges on the profit margins they'd have a stranglehold on a corner of civilization. Then they'd merge with Star Cross or somebody, and another piece of the jigsaw of Galactic Empire would be in place. I wouldn't live to see it, unless I got really unlucky and the whispering thing that rode in my mind let me live forever. Once the amalgamation had taken place Zacher's collection of toy traders would be put to the thankless task of drawing into their net all the little worlds which had stayed out of the loose network of exploitation—the worlds which had contrived, somehow, to look after themselves. Things could get unpleasant then—all around. One by one, they'd be tied in one way or another. There could be no escape *except* ultimate escape—total insularity. Only the Coventry worlds could stay out of the company bag forever—worlds which turned their back on the stars from which the settlers had come, and forgot that there was a great big wonderful universe on their tail end. I could smell wars—maybe a hundred years off, maybe only five. They'd come. It's a great big *fragile* universe.

Sam came down out of the skipper and we set off for the port clearing-house. The sun—a deep red sun—was already close to setting. I had no idea how fast local time might run and I didn't really care. I was still becalmed by the desolation of newfound freedom, and the length of the night didn't seem a terribly relevant thing. I had no ideas, no foci in time. I was content to drift with Sam.

The air was thin but clean and fresh. There was a light wind, perhaps a little cold for comfort, but rolling just a hint of alien odors across the field. It was easy enough, drifting, I thought. I didn't mind the emptiness.

Though I didn't know it, a fragment of darkness from the long shadow of my past was waiting for me in the clearing-house. It hadn't just caught up with me, it was already ahead of me.

We walked into a small coffee-house at the farther end of the huddle of transient-traps which crowded around the field. I just followed Sam, and he went straight there without glancing into any of the lighted windows or advertising displays which edged out on to the pavement along our path as if they were waiting to pounce.

I let him order both food and drink. This was his stamping ground and he was canny enough to have sorted out something that was better than the average.

I hadn't noticed the man waiting at the port while our papers were checked, and I hadn't consciously realized that we'd been followed from the clearing-house.

When we sat down, I asked Sam why the kid had called him Turpin.

"They all do," he said. "It's an old joke. Old and tired. But you know how these things live and never die."

"What was the punchline?" I inquired.

"I always had a yen to be a highwayman. Dick Turpin. When I was a kid I wanted to grow up to be a space pirate. I guess the joke stayed with me since I was so high. I talk about it still, sometimes. It's my joke at my expense, I guess. They all pick it up. Hold up a liner and rob it . . . it's a nice idea."

"Not very practical," I commented.

"So who cares? It's a nice idea. Someday, I may give it a try. Just for the laugh."

"Hasn't it ever been done?"

"Who knows?"

"You've never done it."

"No," he said, straight-faced. "I never did. You know how it is. A kid never grows up to be what he's cut out to be. He always gets hammered into some other slot.

Mine's the slot in a drive-unit, any kind and all kinds. But it wouldn't be the same anyway—the dreaming and the doing. Kids can hold up liners, not grown men. I guess it'd be a disappointment."

It was a crazy conversation, but I didn't mind it. I was about to pursue the point further when I became conscious of the fact that someone was standing behind me. Sam was looking up at him, and the light crept under those ashen eyebrows to shine off his eyes.

I turned around.

"Mr. Grainger," he said.

I looked at him, and I could feel my stomach sinking. I didn't know him from Adam, but I knew his style. I recognized immediately what he represented. Something from behind me, treading on my heels. He knew me. And he wasn't an autograph hunter.

"Never heard of him," I said.

"Me neither," lied Sam, unthinkingly.

"I was at the port," he said, smoothly and gently. "I saw your papers checked."

"So? The galaxy is brim full of men named Grainger. The one you want is one of the other ten thousand. Try the slums on Penaflor."

"I'd like to talk to you, if I may," he said. Some people just can't take a hint.

He was tall, and though he stood quite relaxed he was neat enough and straight enough to suggest that he had some kind of discipline in his background. I knew he wasn't a cop and I knew he wasn't a New Alexandrian. He was dark haired but pale skinned, and he had just a hint of makeup in the mold of his face. He talked with a silky catch to his voice which suggested that English wasn't his first or his only language. His coat was expensive and behind his collar I could see the sharp white of a good shirt. I looked down at his shoes, knowing that they'd be shiny. If I'd been Sherlock Holmes I would have known his pet poodle's nickname, but as things stood I only knew that he was trouble.

"No," I said.

"Just a few words," he said calmly. He wasn't bothering to sound friendly. Just confident.

"I don't want to know," I said. "I'm not interested. I just don't care. Go away."

"We care," he said. He pulled a chair out from one of the other tables and he sat down wrong way around, so that his hands could rest on the back of it, just beside me. He didn't so much as glance at Sam. I knew I was going to have to listen. I didn't see a lot of alternatives.

The waitress brought out the food. Sam looked at her and gave her a nice smile. She knew him by sight and she smiled right back at both of us. I couldn't raise an eyebrow. She probably didn't form too high an opinion of me. I picked up my fork and began to eat. Sam grinned at me, and followed suit.

"I want to offer you a job, Mr. Grainger," said the stranger. "My name is Soulier, and I represent the Caradoc Company. There's nothing underhanded about this—nothing at all. I'm not trying to trick you in any way. You know that we've had an interest in you for some time and we both know what sort of an interest that is. You're a free agent now and we're approaching you as a free agent. We aren't going to pretend that we owe you anything for what happened in the past, but on the other hand, we don't expect you to bury all your grievances for nothing. We need men with your knowledge and experience, Mr. Grainger, and we're willing to pay a good deal over the odds for your services."

I said nothing. He waited for a few seconds and then he went on.

"We are prepared to forget the past, Mr. Grainger, so far as you have contributed to . . . matters disadvantageous to the company. We are prepared to learn from the past. We always like to learn from our mistakes. You know that you have cost us money, and you no doubt feel that there is some justice in that, in view of what happened a year ago when one of our ships picked you up in the Halcyon Drift. You know that we are big enough to shrug off these matters as a drop in the commercial ocean. There need be no resentment between us unless you insist that it should be so . . . and I believe that you are realistic enough not to allow petty prejudices to interfere with your future well-being. We do not hold you responsible in any way for what happened to the ramrods which we lost in the Halcyon core, and we feel that you should be prepared to understand and forgive the unfortunate affair of the *Ella Marita* and the salvage claim. Time has moved on since then. Things happen quickly in the universe today. We want to start again, and we want you with us instead of against us.

"We will give you a ship . . . virtually any type of ship you care to specify . . . yours to command as long as you care to. We are prepared to negotiate freely as to conditions of employment and the nature of the work you will undertake. On your joining the company we will pay you a lump sum to offset any resentment which you may harbor as regards our past clashes. This, too, is negotiable."

"No," I said.

"I'll take it," volunteered Sam. Soulier didn't favor him with so much as a glance.

"We need you, Mr. Grainger," said Soulier, who apparently never tired of flogging dead horses, "and we're being absolutely honest about that. Write your own ticket. Name your price. You don't have to sign on. We'll employ you on any basis whatsoever. Just say the word."

I continued eating, and he continued waiting. He thought I was thinking it over. I wasn't.

—You're in a spot, said the wind.

That I knew.

—You could have guessed that something of this sort might happen.

How could I? I retorted. I'm only a little guy. I'm only a pilot. How could I know the vultures would gather over me the moment I stepped out from under Charlot's perch? Why shouldn't they just let me fade away? What makes me so bloody popular?

—You're too modest, said the wind ominously. Far too modest.

"I don't suppose," I said to Soulier, "that it would do any good to tell you that I don't know anything. Nothing worth your while. I don't know about Charlot's secrets, Charlot's plans, Charlot's methods. I'm not privy to his innermost thoughts and I never have been. I'm only the most minor of his pawns. I'm not a fool and I know what you're asking for, but I couldn't give it to you if I wanted to. You're wasting your time. Now you got an explanation, which I didn't owe you, so will you please go away."

He had frozen up just a bit. I wasn't trying to be nasty. I wasn't being tough. I knew the score and I was outpointed every way. But he thought I was playing hero, and he was all ready to play by the roughest rules.

"Come on, Mr. Grainger," he said gently. "You've been closer to Titus Charlot than anyone else these last few months. You're a clever man, and you aren't one of his disciples by any means. You've been around on New Alexandria, you've flown the *Hooded Swan*, and you've been at the very heart of several incidents which are pregnant with interest so far as our company is concerned. You're a very valuable man, Mr. Grainger. You know that your dreams of avarice aren't big enough to cut much of a hole in company assets. You interest us greatly, Mr. Grainger, and we can afford to indulge that interest. Think of me, if you like, as Caradoc's opposite number to your last employer. A picker-up of loose ends, a dabbler in small projects, but a man with power nevertheless. A man with determination. You don't have to take a job with us at all, if you don't want to. But we want a few days— perhaps only a few hours—of your valuable time, and we're willing to pay you a great deal for it. We just want your memoirs, that's all."

"I've got a very bad memory," I told him.

"In this day and age," he pointed out, "nobody has to rely on the infallibility of his memory."

"You aren't augMENTing me," I said flatly.

"You make augMENTation sound like some kind of torture," he said. "You know that isn't so. It doesn't hurt, and it leaves you just as it finds you, with your memory sharpened up a bit. It's not like a mindpick, you know . . . not at all.

"I know you have secrets, Mr. Grainger . . . haven't we all. But how much can those secrets really be worth? We'll pay it, whatever it is. And your personal secrets mean little enough to us—it's not your private life we're interested in. You have no loyalty to Charlot—he *used* you. He may not have been responsible for your initial troubles but he certainly took the fullest advantage of them. You owe nothing to anyone save yourself. You have a perfect right to sell us all you know, moral and legal. I appreciate your resentment of the augMENTation procedures, but really . . . when you come down to it, is there anything you have to hide? We'll deal honestly, Mr. Grainger—it's not worth our while to be dishonest. Whatever safeguards you care to specify . . . all we want is information. We bear you no malice. None at all."

"I *don't* want to have my memory sharpened," I said. "I'm very good at forgetting because I *like* forgetting. There are some things I don't care to remember at *any* price."

There was another pause. I finished my meal. Sam was already finished. I guess I'd been distracted somewhat.

"You don't look to me like a man who doesn't want to be rich," said Soulier. "It's just not your line. You don't want to end your days dragging a heap like the *Sandman* around the radiant rim. You want a ship of your own. Maybe a world of your own. It can be arranged. You can't afford to turn us down, Mr. Grainger. It wouldn't be fair to yourself." That was a threat if I ever heard one, though it lacked any kind of inflection.

The food was fine but I was feeling sick. My stomach was all churned up. I wanted this man off my back and I wanted him off fast, but I knew there was no way. If the company had made up its commercial collective mind—and it seemed that it had—there was simply no way to say no.

"Soulier," I said, "I wouldn't sell you my soul for the entire assets of your goddamned company and I don't care if it *does* end up owning the universe. Don't get me wrong . . . it isn't loyalty or pride or even downright bloody-mindedness. It's simple fear. I don't trust you as far as I can throw a feather into a gale-force headwind, and I'd be every kind of fool if I did. You can't have my mind, Soulier. Not for all your promises and not for any of your threats. No way. I've got legal rights, here and everywhere I mean to go, and I've got Titus Charlot on the end of a call for help. You can't take my mind, Soulier, and I think that you can get that message into your skull if you work hard enough. No counterthreats—I'm just telling you the plain truth. It's not me that'll stop you, it's the bounds of possibility."

Soulier rocked back in his chair, picking its back legs up off the floor. I hoped he'd fall over.

"I haven't made any threats," he said evenly—and it was the most threatening sound *I'd* ever heard. "I'm only in-

terested in honest dealing. The company is only interested
in honest dealing. We're trying to establish contact with
you, so that we can *both* get what we want.

"You know that you're finished with Charlot and vice
versa. You're on your own. You *know* that. I think you
should accept our offer. I think you will. It's an *honest*
offer, Mr. Grainger, and it will stay that way. We only
want to make you a rich man. I want you to understand
that."

"Yeah," I said. "I understand." One of us was lying
and it wasn't me.

"I'll be in town for some days," said Soulier. "At the
organization's hotel. Anyone will tell you which it is. Ask
for Mr. Zacher. You can contact me through him, any
time."

"I'll be gone in two days," I told him.

"Will you, Mr. Grainger?" he said flatly.

I hate people who call me "mister."

"Good-bye, Mr. Grainger," he said, as he stood up and
replaced the chair neatly. "I'll be waiting to hear from
you."

Then he left.

I felt Sam Parks's eyes boring into the top of my head
as I stared down at my empty plate and turned my fork
over and over, clicking the tines against the plastic rim.

"You know," he said, "ever since I was so high, I've
had this thing about the romantic life of high crime. I guess
I never had any real ambition."

"Honestly," I said, to no one in particularly, "I didn't
think I was worth it. I *don't* think I'm worth it. Bloody
hell, I'm *not* worth it. They steal my mind they may get
a lot of things they didn't bargain for; but mother is it
worth it? It's all just trash. Why can't the bloody universe,
just for a while, get off my back?"

"Take the money," advised Sam.

"I can't," I said.

"They might just let you keep it," he said. "I'd take it."

"It's not the money," I told him. "If there was a chance
of getting away with it, I might, but . . . "

"No chance?"

"They don't like me. Can you, in your heart of hearts,
see the Caradoc Company lending a piece of string to

someone they don't like, let alone giving him money? It's not the way the world works. They can afford to pay off their petty grudges."

"Yes," he said. "I guess they can."

There were three of them, and they were big.

Sam was still with me. We'd had a few drinks and we'd had a stroll, and we talked. Mostly about space and space-faring. Nothing exciting. Nothing important. Nothing about the sad and sorry mess. When it came time for Sam's turn to mind the baby we set out for the ship. The softening squad was waiting by the gate to the field.

They were obviously local talent, hired to do a little of what they might well be doing anyhow, on their own account, to somebody else. They weren't really there for the purpose of hurting me—though they would. Nor were they there in order to persuade me to listen to Caradoc's brand of reason. They were just there to drop a hint, to let me know that what I already knew was not only true but inescapable.

They didn't want to take us in the middle of the street, so they came shuffling out of the shadows with the intention of herding us down a convenient alley before working us over. I took a couple of quick steps back, and they moved like lightning to cut me off, but I maneuvered myself into the blaze of the lights, into the center-street pool of glare from the clip joints and the neon signs. I wasn't going to let them have their party in private.

There were people on the street, flitting back and forth. But they moved swiftly, without any hint of a glance in my direction, and pretended to be shadows.

There was music—loud, fast, drum-beating—oozing out of the fun-parlors on either side. The street was only twelve feet wide, but the music seemed to be coming from a vast distance. Nevertheless, I found myself thinking in time to it as I stopped in my tracks, and the twanging of the guitars was oddly noticeable. I had half a dozen shadows sprawling across the smooth street—some pink, some green.

"Get out of it, Sam," I said. "They might not bother with you."

"Ha!" he muttered. "You they do for the drop. I'm thrown in as a bonus. Tonight's special offer. Besides, there are only three of them."

They stood still, mocking us with their coolness and their fake mafia stances. Sam knew as well as I did that we didn't stand a chance. Not even if there were only two.

"Run," I said.

"Don't be a fool."

They were wallowing in their anticipation as they swayed forward like a trio of ballet-dancing bulldozers. They were letting the tension build up to snapping point.

It snapped, and in they came.

I knew that it was no good trying to get away, and I made up my mind that I was going to hit one of them a blow he'd feel. But when the first boot went into my gut I knew that there wasn't going to be any gesture of defiance. I tried one desperate kick that didn't have any real chance of mashing anybody's balls, and then I began to fold up. I hid my face with one arm and my nether regions with the other hand, and I let them knock me sideways toward the light-streaming window on my left.

I was brought up against the plate-glass so hard that when my ear came away again I thought for one ungodly moment I'd cracked it and they were going to send me crashing through it to slash myself to ribbons in the debris.

Somebody said *"Get the bastards!"* in a voice full of hatred and loathing, and for a crazy instant I wondered how they came to be hating me on top of it all. I just couldn't understand why anyone should be so goddamn *mean*. Then I realized that it was the heavy mob who were getting got, and getting got in no uncertain terms. With some considerable shock I realized that it was the kid from the ship who had spoken the magic words—the kid whose name I didn't even know. He wasn't alone.

It was at least ten against three, and I have to confess that it was a pretty enough sight from where I was sitting. I'm by no means a violent man, but I can lie down beside the nastiest fight and not get a bit upset if those who are suffering have harbored nasty thoughts toward me.

Nasty thoughts they had certainly harbored, but thanks to providence they hadn't done me any lasting damage. Sam Parks helped me up from where I'd slid down the window.

"Cretins," he said, mumbling slightly because someone had hit him hard on the side of his mouth. "I been on this road all my life. There isn't a door on thirty-two worlds I can't yell 'help' into and not get it."

"Thanks, Sam," I said.

"Don't thank me," he said. "Thank the guys who answered. But they'll be glad enough to help. Spacemen, handlers—even port officers—they all come in for a bit of hammer from the local delinquents from time to time. Look at them . . . you can see they're enjoying themselves. A bit of their own back for most, I guess."

The fight seemed to be growing. A lot of people seemed to want a bit of their own back.

"I think the locals got reinforcements," I said.

"It wouldn't be polite to leave," he pointed out.

I saw his point, but I didn't see much point in staggering back into the fray. I might end up just as badly mauled as the vicious threesome had initially intended. It was hard to decide how much time I could, in all decency, spend sagging back against the window looking pained, but I was saved the embarrassment of having to show my gratitude and comaraderie by further participation when the police turned up.

Within minutes the street was empty of all but honest spacemen and their friends. No arrests seemed likely to be made, and everyone seemed quite unworried about the whole affair. I thanked the kid, honestly and sincerely. He looked glad to have been of assistance, and pretty proud of himself. So far as I was concerned, he was welcome.

Sam and I continued on our weary way back to the *Sandman*.

"You're hot," he said.

"I know," I told him.

"There's going to be more trouble," he predicted dolefully.

I knew that too, and I said so.

"If there's anything I can do . . . " he said, without any extraordinary enthusiasm.

"There's no point in sticking your neck out along with mine," I told him. "Don't get involved with Caradoc. It hurts. There's only one man can get me out of this and I'm not sure that he'd bother. Come to that, I'm not sure if the cure is much better than the disease. If I could reach him, which I can't."

"You want me to send a message?"

"It'd take weeks to get where it has to go. Things are a bit more imminent than that, I really feel. If we can lift off tomorrow, maybe I can gain the time to get things sorted out so Charlot will get them off my back. But if we can't . . . "

I left it hanging, which was how I felt.

We got back to the ship without encountering any more trouble, and the officer who was watching it while the captain was hunting up contacts let us in. We went up to the cockpit and set the screen to give us a view of the distant port offices.

"You got a gun?" asked Sam.

"Never owned one in my life," I told him.

"Draw one from the locker," he advised. "I'll make sure Haeckel OK's it in the morning."

I shook my head.

He sprawled in one of the couches, fiddling with the straps and eyeing me dourly.

"We could—" he said, and trailed off.

"Go on," I prompted.

His lips formed the word "lift," but there was barely any sound behind it.

"Oh sure," I said, trying not to sound too derisory. "Just you and me. Off into the unknown. That's a crime, you know. Mutiny, theft . . . there must be more. Never to set foot in any recognized port again. Alien worlds and the backsides of maverick colonies. It's a great life for the congenitally lonely."

"It's been done," he said quietly, shielding himself from the halfhearted sarcasm.

"It's been done," I agreed. "But not so often. It's easy. Sometimes it's downright attractive. But you know the score, Sam, even if you never kicked around on alien worlds and never made an illicit landing in your life.

Sure, no port authority has a hope in hell of controlling all traffic in and out of its territory. But the system works . . . just how are we supposed to make a living in a tin can like this? How do we pay for the fuel? It isn't the bounds of possibility that has us caged, Sam, it's the money. Money is a medium of exchange . . . and it has to *be* exchanged. That's where you can't break the system . . . right there. The law couldn't catch us, but that doesn't mean we'd get away. Thanks for the offer."

I won't say I wasn't tempted. I'm no lover of port authority and carrying papers and doing everything the right way, but I'd had experience. Years of it. Lapthorn was always trying to get beyond human reach, to cast himself—and me—adrift, to become a real citizen of the galaxy instead of just a human invader. It's just not that simple. I understand the urge to be a highwayman, to abandon all responsibility and cast off all repression, and I sympathize. I really do. But it's only a dream, and no matter where the rim is said to be the sticky fingers of civilization can reach you just so long as you're trying to operate with six thousand tons of very complicated, very expensive human technology wrapped around you. Space may offer unlimited freedom, but you can't collect unless you can do without a spaceship. That's the way it is.

—Nevertheless, the wind chipped in, it *has* been done.

Don't remind me, I said.

Meanwhile, the silence was hanging a little heavy on Sam's hands. He felt that he was involved in this, somehow. I'd known him only a matter of days, and most of our business had been transacted through a call circuit, but already he was as close to me as Lapthorn had ever been. I was letting him stand that close, and I knew it. By not reacting to his presence I was slowly sucking him into my problem. A year ago, I couldn't have let that happen.

After a while, he said, "What are you going to do?"

I didn't know. I thought that was obvious. What was there to be done?

"There's only one thing you can do, you know," he said.

"I'm not going to hijack the ship," I said, "and I'm not going to shoot it out. I'm not Dick Turpin, I'm not Billy the Kid, and I'm not Flash Gordon."

"It's either run into space," he said, with an all too accurate assessment of the probable alternatives, "or run on the ground. You can't dodge a man like that standing still."

His logic was devastating. I had this slender thread of hope which stretched n thousand light-years to the long arm of Titus Charlot and the New Alexandrian puppet-masters, but no gambler would ever put his loose change on a chance like that, let alone his shirt and all its contents. I had to reckon to be on my own, and if I was on my own I had to start thinking rabbit. It was either space or dirt. Sam was on my side, and if I could only reach Captain Haeckel's hard heart maybe a run for the stars was on—semi-legally, at least. But if Haeckel *wasn't* on the side of the angels . . . if he even remained neutral . . .

And we had to remember that it wasn't Haeckel's ship. He was an employee, not an entrepreneur. And I knew from the way he chewed his gum that he hadn't spent *his* boyhood dreaming about the day he was going to cut loose and become a highwayman. He was nobody's sucker, and his best friend would never accuse him of being a hero. No serious student of probability would back Haeckel. No way. So what was I left with?

Mud.

"It's not a bad world," said Sam, meaning it was god-awful. "The colony hasn't ever really got off the ground, but you know damn well that the way the billions scattered, no colony ever had a fair chance without luck or a bonanza." That was true enough, I guessed—the old overpopulation neurosis and the back-to-the-trees brigade had contrived to spread the human race as thin as butter in an Earthside sandwich.

"It's rough out beyond the port complex," said Sam, "but that might be all to the good from your point of view."

"I'm no backwoodsman," I told him sourly. "I'm not the type to go traipsing out into nowhere to build myself a log cabin, plant potatoes, and trap the local equivalent of the squirrel. It's not my life. I'm a machine-man. I'm a starman, and you can't be a starman without living so close to machines you become fifty percent printed circuit yourself. If nothing else, I've proved *that* in my long and checkered past. I spent two years on the side of a mountain haunting the ruins of a shattered starships, and it was every single day too long. It's not my life. It's just no kind of life at all."

"It's not forever," said Sam. "The heat never lasts forever. They'd lose interest in you . . . how fast? A year? A month? This bird has better things to do than hang around here waiting for you to surface. How can he search a world?"

He was right, of course. Unless I wanted to face out Soulier—and I'd have to be crazy to do that—I had to take a long walk in the wilderness. My memory kept flashing back to the long blur in my history that was two tormented years on a bleak black rock. Here, there were trees. But it was still cold, still wild, still empty. I stared the prospect in the face, but it wasn't an easy one to look at steadily. Two years of sitting in on my own death-watch had provided me with one hell of a distaste for the simple life.

No doubt I could survive it, but could I face it?

How about you, sunbeam? I asked. What's your solution?

—You got it all taped, he said. There's nothing to add.

It must be the first time, I commented bitterly.

—I'm only a tactician, he said. I could have won you the fight if you hadn't been so determined to play tortoise. I can keep you alive till tomorrow. Say the word and we'll go to war with Soulier. But you're the strategist. It's your body and your life. You live it the way you choose to live it. You need help, you call me, and it's yours. But you and I have both learned a lot from trying to fit together. I'm hurling no insults, I'm making no comments. I'll go along with you.

That I suppose, testified to the fact that I'd won some kind of victory in the months of my freedom. I'd won respect from my mind parasite. One time, he'd been ever-ready to tell me exactly how to take the next hurdle—and ever-ready to take it himself if I was ready to cop out. I'd learned from him, he from me. We were running the race together now.

It didn't help the decision, but if he'd offered advice it wouldn't have helped either. It would have sidetracked the whole issue. This way, I was still poised. Devil or deep blue sea?

"It pays to stay alive," said Sam.

"I'm not going to let Soulier have his way," I said. "Of all things, that's the top priority. I can't fight Caradoc, but I'm damned if I'll let them crush me. I'll go to hell first, let alone the backwoods. They made me an offer I can't refuse."

"That's the worst kind," agreed Sam.

"So bugger 'em. I'll cheat the bastards if it kills me."

Trouble was, it might.

My stomach had never recovered from the sinking it took when I first found the man from Caradoc standing at my shoulder, and the gut-blow it took from the heavy hadn't helped any. If it wasn't for the wind I could have had a hellish case of indigestion. In spite of the wind, I felt one coming on.

Then the call circuit beeped. It sounded like I felt.

I automatically reached out to answer it, but Sam was up off his couch knocking my hand away. "I'm O.O.W.," he muttered. "Want to get me shot?"

He acknowledged the call, and I heard the captain's voice interrupt him, in a cold, syrupy tone.

"You get that drive-unit into shape," he said. "Wake Grainger. I've got the others here and I'm bringing them in. Plus a couple of passengers. We've been chartered and we're taking off tonight. As soon as humanly possible. These guys have pressing business."

"We can't," Sam protested. "Half the cargo is still underneath our fins. They knocked off shifting it when their time ran out. Where you going to find a gang at this time of night? Or is the kid going to do it all himself?"

"The gang is on its way out right now," said the captain. "The area will be clear in ninety minutes. We've been cleared for takeoff already. We lift at oh-oh-six ship-standard. Move it."

"Yes, Captain Haeckel, sir," said Sam, with more than a hint of insubordination, "you're the boss."

He switched off the circuit, and he turned his pale eyes on me.

"They found out you're not in the hospital," he said. "You just ran right out of time. If you're going to run, you better start right now. They'll be covering the port, but there are ways of getting through the perimeter. . . ."

My legs were itching. For all I knew they might be underneath the fins right now, with a butterfly net, just waiting. I looked at the screen, and I saw half a dozen tiny figures ambling across the tarpol. The jumbo crew. No Haeckel, no passengers.

"I'm on my way," I said.

"I'll come with you," said Sam.

"What the hell *for*?"

He was already on his way out of the door, running for his cabin.

"I'll show you the way through the perimeter," he called back.

"Man," I said, "I know how to skip a field. I'm not an idiot."

But he'd gone. He was coming. I knew he was a fool, and that it wouldn't do him or me the slightest bit of good. I knew that he didn't and shouldn't owe me anything, and that he was riding the tide of some ridiculous impulse. But I didn't have the heart to stop him. I didn't *want* to stop him.

"Thanks, Sam." I said, as I moved to the door myself. He couldn't hear me. I was talking to myself.

IV

I grabbed my packsack, which contained virtually nothing except some clothes and some junk (eyeshades, a few tools, a miniature medical kit), and I didn't pause to say good-bye to my ship. Sam spent a couple of minutes rummaging in his bunk locker and in his engine room, filling up his pockets with anything that looked potentially useful. Then we slipped out of the belly of the ship into the shadow of the fins. The cargo, unevenly distributed over an area of thirty or forty square yards, gave us some cover while we dodged away from the ship and hared across the field.

The gang of laborers who were trucking out toward us didn't see us, and we didn't see anyone else skulking in the shadows. Soulier shouldn't have let Haeckel call the ship. It was a mistake—I thought. We made it through the perimeter fence and into the bush without the slightest suspicion of trouble. We got clear of the environs in a matter of minutes.

We were out of breath, but we didn't stop. We pushed ourselves on into the darkness.

At first we were traveling across land where human feet had undoubtedly trod and trod often. Several times we skirted fields where the locals were trying to persuade things to grow or rear meat animals. The only thing which attempted to get in our way at any time was a cow. It must have sensed that I didn't like cows, because it thought better of it when we came too close.

Eventually, however, we got out into some real wild country—moor and scrub. When dawn came we were dog tired, and making very little progress across the countryside. When gray daylight came the wind seemed sharper and the air seemed colder. It was crystal clear.

There wasn't a hint of mist close to the ground or cloud up in the sky. The big red sun was a long time dragging himself up over the horizon, and even when he was pushing on clear into the sky it didn't seem to get any warmer.

We'd stopped running, but we kept on making what pace we could. Sam moved with surprising ease and tirelessness—I think he was trading on a certain excitement and the sheer hell of it. It was largely desperation that kept my feet going.

We didn't pause until we hit the road. Sam was pleased when we did and he reckoned we ought to follow it. At least we'd know we were going somewhere, and we shouldn't find it too difficult to make ourselves unobtrusive if someone happened along that we'd rather not meet.

I trusted his judgment, and it made walking a little easier.

We ended up sometime after noon in a vast complex of fields which were in the process of being marked out for management on a grand scale. Some of the land was cleared, some of it was already under cultivation, but there were signs that this was quite an old plan which had somehow failed to get off the ground completely. It suggested optimism rather than determination. There was equipment lying around on the edges of fields which nature was in the process of reinvading, and it was both old and dilapidated. A big bulldozer sat on the crest of a ridge nearly half a mile away, looking functional enough, but this was someone's unrealized dream, not the lifeblood of a world. From the crest of that same rise, when we reached it, we could see the whole scope of the project and get the feel of its hollowness. The land was dotted with long, low huts and barns that looked like slices cut off a railway tunnel, semicircular in section. In one of these we stopped for our first rest, and to catch up on some of the sleep we'd missed out on the night before.

It wasn't provided with all the comforts of home, but among the paraphernalia which some kind person had left behind—a long time before, to judge by the dust— was a heating unit and some moldy sugar. Sam had some coffee, and when all the resources were pooled we had the foundation of a hot meal.

The simple victory of being able to heat and sweeten

some gruel, and to wash down the sticky stuff with a cup of coffee made me feel a great deal better. Such small things can make an appreciable difference to one's ability to look inevitable misfortune squarely in the eyes.

We went to sleep.

They arrested us before we woke up and ran us in for jumping ship and leaving port without authorization. Under the law, that made us liable for the smallest of fines, and it seemed an awful lot of trouble for the cops to have gone to. But they knew exactly where to find us. It was only a matter of driving out in a jeep.

They actually handcuffed us before carrying us back to town.

We had to share a cell because there were only two, and until we came in both contained some poor unfortunate who was still sleeping off the night before. We couldn't expect that they'd put real desperadoes like us in with harmless individuals like that, so they let one of the drunks go home. He left his smell behind, though.

The cops never vouchsafed more than a couple of grunts in reply to any of my witty comments or polite questions. They were just doing what came naturally.

We didn't have long to wait for visitors. Haeckel and Soulier came together. Not quite hand-in-hand, but almost.

Haeckel thanked the cops very kindly and explained that he probably wouldn't want to press charges once he'd talked it over with us, but he'd like to give them a little present to compensate them for their trouble and demonstrate due appreciation for all their most welcome cooperation.

They took the gratuity without a murmur, all in the course of the day's work. They knew that it wasn't the captain's money, and they knew that next time he was on Erica he'd be as likely to spit in their eye and howl at them for letting dogs shit in the street, but the first thing that you learn in police school is not to be surprised at the weird ways of the world. Cops have to take things calmly. They accepted the cash philosophically and collected the keys to the cell.

Soulier, meanwhile, ambled over to the cell and favored me with a patronizing smile. His face looked even more artificial in the daylight, but it wasn't anywhere near as artificial as his benign expression.

"I put a tag on you," he said. "While I was standing beside you in the crumb parlor. Before you even noticed I was there. You've been radiating like an electric skunk ever since."

"You can't win 'em all," I said venomously.

"You can't win," he said.

I'd already figured that out. I didn't bother to offer him any further opportunity to gloat. The fact that I hadn't guessed about the tap before I started running left a bad taste in my mouth. I felt like a mug. Being gathered into the gaping jaws of Caradoc was one thing, being made a monkey was quite something else. At that particular moment I almost felt worse about the recent past than I did about the imminent future.

When they unlocked the door I felt a truly powerful temptation to smash one or two of Soulier's pretty-white teeth into the back of his throat. I quelled it. It wasn't the gentlemanly thing to do, and he'd only go and buy some more.

As I walked out, Haeckel grinned at Sam, and gave me a peculiar look that I couldn't quite decipher. Maybe it was something like an apology for having rowed in with my nemesis. Perhaps it had some sadness because he was losing a great pilot and gaining only a mittful of filthy lucre. Perhaps there was also some amusement there, because I was a poor fool.

"You shouldn't have done it, Sam," he said. He was prepared to be friendly. Half-friendly at least.

"Bug off," said Sam, perhaps unwisely. He wasn't feeling friendly at all. He was feeling deflated. He obviously realized that he was overstepping the mark, because he amended himself in a lower voice: "I mean, bug off, *sir*." The comment was directed inward, as though he were reprimanding himself for forgetting the addition.

"If you want to stay here *that* bad," said Haeckel, evenly but without any remaining trace of the fake bonhomie, "I can get along without you. A kid of six could push that engine as well as you."

"Yes, Captain," said Sam. He sounded rather tired.

"Shall we go?" said Soulier.

And then the door opened. I don't think I've ever been

more pleased to see anyone in all my life. Maybe if it
had been Titus Charlot himself, or even Nick delArco,
my delight would have been tempered by a feeling that
I'd been maneuvered right back into the net without my
feet even touching the ground, and that Soulier was only a
pawn in a greater game. But it was Denton. A man who
stood not only for New Alexandrian cunning, but for
New Roman law.

Denton was a guy who could be liked.

"I thought you weren't going to make it," I said.

Neither Haeckel nor Sam Parks had realized that the
situation was materially changed, because Denton was
wearing a police uniform, and people in police uniforms
do have a tendency to walk in and out of police stations
all the time. But the local cops were under no such illusion, and Soulier suddenly looked very, very nasty indeed.

The man who'd accepted the notes from Haeckel, and
who still had the cash clasped in his clammy little hand,
was a bright crimson color.

"This is quite amazing," said Denton suavely. "I hardly
thought that you'd have arrested the man before I arrived
with the warrant."

The blushing man let his jaw drop slightly, and then he
began to gather himself together.

But Soulier wasn't going to hang around while this thing
was sorted right out from under his nose. He cut in before
the cop had got halfway through identifying himself, and
interposed his bulk between Denton and the desk.

"Who the hell do you think you are?" he demanded. All
my illusions were shattered. He'd seemed such a nice,
clever, self-controlled man.

"I'm Commander Denton," said my rescuer—he appeared to have come in for some fast promotion. "I have
a warrant for the apprehension of a man called Grainger."
He dug into his pocket and brought out a gray envelope.
Soulier reached for it but Denton moved it slickly out of
his reach.

"Who is this man?" he demanded of the desk attendant.

"You know damn well who I am," said Soulier. "And
you can't have Grainger. He's been arrested for jumping
ship and he has to stand trial here."

"The charge was dropped," I put in.

"No it wasn't," said Haeckel, who appeared to have

caught on to the fact that he was about to wake up from his dream of avarice. "I only said I *might* drop it when I thought it over. The charges stand."

"He bribed the cop, too," I said. Not that it was relevant, but I felt that it might help the discussion along.

Denton reached out his hand and eased Soulier to one side. He presented the warrant to the man at the desk and said, "I demand that you release the man called Grainger into my custody instantly. Whether or not he has committed a minor offense on this world is quite immaterial. You'll find that my warrant takes precedence. If you care to check the papers you'll find everything in order. You may, if you wish, apply for him to be extradited from New Alexandria in order to face charges here, once he has been tried there."

"I'll have to check with the chief," said the desk cop.

"Do it now," said Denton.

"Yes, sir," said the cop, and moved back from the desk into the small room where the communications panel was situated. Denton moved past Soulier to stand in front of me. Haeckel took an instinctive step backward. Soulier suddenly looked rather isolated in the middle of the floor.

"I thought you were Titus Charlot's bodyguard," I said.

"Promotion," he told me. "I'm an odd-job man now."

"So Titus wants me home."

Denton shook his head slightly. "Titus doesn't want Caradoc to get a tape of your memory. He feels that it would embarrass him. We could hardly have anticipated anything along these lines, but nobody can keep anything secret these days. We caught on, and we moved as fast as we could."

"You came out in the *Swan*?"

He shook his head. "The *Swan*'s in dry dock," he said. "Not in use. No crew. Titus has the sister ship up in the air now, and he's taken it for a little spin around the inner rim. Place called Darlow. Observation and experiment. You know it?"

I'd never heard of it, and I said so. I asked him exactly what was going to happen to me once he got me off Erica and away from Caradoc.

Soulier came back in at this point. "I'd like to hear the answer to that as well," he said. "This man is an employee of the Caradoc Company."

"Like hell I am," I protested.

"Yes you are," he insisted. "We bought your ship."

"Haeckel said you chartered it!" We both turned to the captain for confirmation.

"We own it," said Soulier definitely. "Don't we, Captain?"

Haeckel hesitated, openmouthed.

"It's not his to sell," Sam intervened. "He can't sell it."

"He's the authorized agent of his owners," said Soulier smoothly. "And he sold the ship to me on their behalf last night. For thirty-five thousand." He looked at Haeckel like a snake hypnotizing a rabbit.

Haeckel's eyes flickered away, resting first on my face and then on Denton's. He licked his lips and weighed his chances, while everybody waited to hear what he had to say.

"You bought it," he said, and then added, "for *forty-five* thousand."

Soulier looked as if he wanted to kick the captain in the face.

"Moron," commented Sam. He put his face close to my ear and whispered, "That extra ten thou will go to the owners. He'd have got more kickback from Soulier than he will from *them*." I agreed with him. Haeckel was a bit of an idiot.

"It makes no difference who the *hell* owns the ship," I said. "I resign. I'm entitled."

"Can't you understand," said Denton, who sounded tired in the face of all this desperate wrangling, "that it doesn't matter at all. It makes not the slightest difference. He's under arrest and he's going back to New Alexandria with me. Things can be sorted out there. Things will *have* to be sorted out there."

I felt like a parcel with an obscure address.

"Any claim," continued Denton, "by the police on this world, or by anyone else, will have to come up to the court at Civitas Solis on New Alexandria. There it will be dealt with properly and legally."

"Want to bet on your chances." I asked Soulier.

"Don't get too cocky," Denton said to me, with a slight edge on his voice. "This law will have to deal with you, too. That warrant's real. You take your chances in court like everybody else. And the law on New Alexandria *doesn't* take bribes, nor does it appreciate your kind of humor. I should temper your exultancy if I were you."

"Thanks a lot," I said. "I love you too."

"Well, then—" said Denton.

The chief of police finally made it through the door, banged it shut, looked around as if wondering which of us to shoot, and then demanded to know why his police station looked more like a railway station.

Denton and Soulier went to sort it out, leaving Sam and Captain Haeckel and myself in the corner. I shrugged, and went back into the cell to sit down. Sam looked at Haeckel, then at me, and he joined me. He shut the door behind him.

The captain stared at us through the bars. "Parks," he said, "you're out of a job."

"Yeah," said Sam, "and you're out of a friend."

"What the *hell* is going on here?" screamed the drunk in the other cell.

I felt suddenly and wonderfully serene. Events had caught up with me and I had no idea at all where it was going to lead—except that I wasn't going to be forcibly augMENTed and have my memories exhibited to all kinds of prying eyes. Even if I was still booked to get my feet blistered I was well clear of the frying pan.

"All go, isn't it?" I commented.

V

———◆———

The chief of police was obviously a man amenable to reason. It didn't take too long to get the situation squared as far as the law on Erica was concerned. No charges were to be preferred against me, or against Sam, and if Caradoc wanted to try to pretend they owned either of us they could do it entirely on their own initiative. All assistance from the local police force was withdrawn. I never did find out what happened to the cash Haeckel gave the desk cop, but I suspect that it didn't find its way back into the Caradoc coffers.

I persuaded Denton that Sam would be a valuable asset to New Alexandria, and that it wouldn't be kind to strand him on Erica. We shipped out together in the fast p-shifter which had brought Denton out on his errand of mercy. It was a really top-class piece of equipment, and I enjoyed the trip. Being in service rather than in private use, every spare cubic foot aboard the ship was crammed with something functional, but nevertheless she was a comfortable ship. The only thing lacking was a space where more than two people could sit down and talk to one another, but I did manage to engage Denton in conversation a couple of times. There were certain things I felt I ought to know.

"You're actually going to put me on trial, aren't you?" I asked him.

"We could hardly do anything else."

"Wasn't there some simpler way to extract me from Soulier's clutches? Brute force, maybe? I know it's not much in New Alexandria's line, but turning me into a criminal is a bit extreme, isn't it?"

"Has it occurred to you," he said, "that we didn't come all the way out here for the pleasure of saving your hide?

40

Hasn't it filtered through to your brain that Titus Charlot might just be pig sick of you? Might it not have occurred to you that the safest way of keeping the contents of your mind safe from enemy hands would be to lock you up for the rest of your miserable life?"

"Are you serious?" I demanded. I was absolutely aghast.

"Not wholly," he admitted. "But don't fall into the trap of assuming you have a guardian angel. You're under arrest, and you're going to be tried. Personally, I reckon you'll get off. I don't think the prosecution has a case. But you'll get a fair trial, and that means no bias either way. This isn't a fix, and you'd be wrong to think it was."

"What the hell am I charged with, for God's sake?" I said.

"Kidnapping."

My first impulse was to laugh, but second thoughts caught up quickly. Denton had arrested me once before, on New Alexandria. I'd been joyriding in one one of Charlot's cars and I'd picked up an alien runaway from one of his research establishments. A girl. She'd been running from two guys who looked far more like hustlers than helpmates. They hadn't looked to me like they should be trusted with a dog, so I'd been rather rude to them and refused to let them take the girl. They hadn't been pleased. Neither had Charlot—he'd sent the law out to pick me up. I hadn't enjoyed the affair, and I hadn't liked the picture when it was filled in for me, one way and another, but I thought the incident was well and truly closed. I had been told to mind my own business and that was that. I suppose it was a natural to provide the kind of leverage they wanted to bring me home and out of Caradoc's reach, but it still seemed to be coming down a bit hard.

What's more, technically I might be guilty.

"Wait a minute," I said. "This is all going to be taken seriously? The prosecution is going to try to make it stick?"

"That's right."

"Well, hell," I protested. "It *might*."

"That's what I've been trying to point out."

"What kind of penalty does a charge like that carry?"

"Circumstances alter cases," he pointed out. "You have some extenuating circumstances. They wouldn't throw the book at you."

"I was working for Charlot, too," I said.

"That won't help. But even if you do get convicted—and I reckon you won't—I doubt if you'll get more than a couple of years. Maybe three."

"You're stringing me along, you bastard," I said.

"Don't bet on it."

Secretly, I had every confidence that I wasn't going to go to jail. I knew Titus Charlot. What I was really worried about was the kind of lever this little affair might be turned into. Titus Charlot wasn't the kind of man to forgive and forget when one of his pawns walked off the board—and was pretty unpleasant about it en route. Caradoc wasn't the only group who might bear some kind of grudge against me. If Charlot wanted me back, this was just the kind of trick he might pull. It was exactly in his underhanded style.

Bitterly I said, "We're all still playing the same game, aren't we? I haven't escaped that twenty thousand around my neck at all, have I? I never had a chance to get away, did I? Caradoc wasn't the only vulture standing by. Charlot's going to suck me right back in again, isn't he? Better the devil I know than the devil who might otherwise get me . . . I appreciate that. But it's a filthy game, isn't it? Come on, Denton, you're a reasonable man. I'm being played for a sucker. Still. Once a pawn, always a pawn."

Denton shrugged. "I reckon you take it all too hard," he said. "You get paranoid about it. Take it easy. It's the way things go. Believe me, it's not a vast and intricate plot to steal your soul. Nobody's *that* interested in little old you. You're involved, that's all—and you have to be taken into account. I don't know whether Titus Charlot is mad keen to get you out to the Nightingale Nebula or not, though I'm willing to bet that if he does want you there, he'll get you, one way or another. But if he does want you out there, it's not because he's determined to see you into hell his way. It's because he has a job that needs doing. That's all. The universe isn't out to get you, Grainger. You just happen to be in the way."

"Thanks a lot," I said.

"You're welcome."

"Have *you* ever been told to take a ship into the Halcyon Core as a publicity stunt? Have you ever been told to raise an alien warship from a hole in hell for the sake of public relations? Have you ever been turned into the Caradoc Company's number one bogey man through no fault of your own? Charlot's done me no favors, even if he's been sugar icing on *your* career."

"Look at it this way," said Denton. "If we'd left you loose for Caradoc to pick up, you could be in a *real* mess. Just take this as it comes. Relax."

"What do you want?" I complained. "Gratitude? You didn't exactly *rescue* me. It wasn't for my sake that the U.S. cavalry spaced in with bugles blaring, now was it? I was pulled out because of what I knew, or might know—maybe even just to spite the other side."

He shook his head. "That's not altogether fair," he said. "And you can't blame it all on Charlot's machinations. His organization is involved, sure. It wasn't all my idea. But Charlot is out on the inner rim, light-years from New Alex and light-years from Erica."

"On Darlow," I said. "Looking at the Nightingale Nebula. What for? There aren't any lost ships in there. It's not even impressive. Just a scar in space. What's he doing out there?"

"I don't know."

"You wouldn't. You're only a cop. At least I'm an important pawn."

He shrugged.

"All this," I said, "is enough to drive anyone to despair."

"You're welcome," he said. "I've done my bit."

He rose to depart, obviously not altogether in harmony with my feelings.

"Hey," I said. "Who's going to pay for my lawyer?"

"You are," he said. I should have known.

"You couldn't have charged me with stealing the car, I suppose?" I said. "I mean, that would have meant letting me off light. I supposed it never occurred to you, hey?"

He had to turn back to answer me that one. "That's not an extraditing charge," he said. "But it did occur to me. You're charged with that as well."

I laughed hollowly.

"I still think you'll get off," he said.

"Pigs," I said flatly, "might fly."

Later, I talked to Sam. That was more comforting. Sam

Parks was the only guy I'd been able to have a sensible conversation with in quite some time.

'What do you reckon to do now?" I asked him.

"Stick with you, if it's OK," he answered.

"And if I go to jail? Don't say you'll wait for me, for God's sake. We aren't married."

"I'll pick up something," he said. "If you get off, we can pick up something together. Two men can pull off some tricks one man can't. Maybe someday we can get a ship."

"You're dreaming, Sam," I told him. "You're still dreaming."

"That's right," he said.

"You know," I said, "it'd be just like the last guy I shared a ship with. Michael Lapthorn. A dreamer and a half. I thought he'd drive me crazy."

"Perhaps he did," said Sam.

"And I drove you over the edge," I said. "Is that it? What made you do it, Sam? You're no fool. What makes a man like you suddenly chuck in his hand to cast himself adrift, just to take sides with a no-good bum who thinks the universe has a down on him?"

"I don't know," he said. "It seemed like a good idea at the time."

"And now?"

He looked at me out of those sparkling gray eyes. "I don't know," he said. "But what did I have to lose? I think maybe I'd *like* the universe to have a down on me, to push me like you got pushed. That's not the kid in me talking, it's the old man. In all my years, I don't think deep space ever got around to *noticing* me."

"They say some people have all the luck," I said.

"Yeah," he agreed.

"If ever we find the bastard with our share," I said, "let's kick his teeth in."

VI

The trial was fairly straightforward and by no means long drawn out. I had the dubious pleasure of renewing several old acquaintances, including the two sons-of-bitches who'd riled me in the first place. Their evidence was dilute and completely lacking in malice, as was the police evidence. None of the aliens appeared in person to give evidence, but statements were submitted to the court which described my actions in wholly favorable terms.

I remained suspicious until the jury actually declared their verdict, and I kept feeling a temptation to look over my shoulder. I've heard about being innocent until proved guilty, but this was the first time I'd ever seen it put into practice. Everyone was polite to me and no one seemed to think I'd done the foul deed.

It was really no contest. I left the court without a stain on my character.

There was not the slightest sign of any intervention from Titus Charlot. He, too, had submitted a statement to the court, but it was a simple account of the facts, in no way weighted for or against me. Nobody contacted me.

Caradoc, on the other hand, apparently felt it necessary to make a token gesture. They sent lawyers out to do a bit of wrangling, and though they got hardly anywhere they managed to tie me up in court for some time. *They* were certainly not lacking in genuine twenty-two-carat malice.

It all took time, and—more important—money. I had to live while the mess was being sorted out, and I also needed a lawyer. New Alexandrian accommodation and New Roman expertise are not cheap. Far from it, in fact. The legal costs would be written off, eventually, but in the meantime my reserve of cash—large though it was—

dwindled dramatically. And there was Sam, of course, still with me all the way, who hadn't a penny in the world.

By the time everything was cleared up I was way out of pocket, and there was nothing I could do except hang about and wait for the bureaucratic process to repay the high cost of justice. It was about this time that I began to catch the faint aroma of a nearby rat. If there's one place in the known universe where computers ought to work properly it's New Alexandria, and their bureaucratic process is supposedly the fastest in the galaxy. But time dragged by, and I was waiting. I wasn't in desperate straits by any means. Nobody refused me credit. But I was be-calmed—trapped by a gossamer-light web of financial involvement.

Also, the prospects of getting a job looked bleak. It wasn't so much the fact that there were no jobs to be had, but rather that there was a surfeit of unreasonably tempting offers. The Caradoc Company was just dying to employ me, directly, indirectly, or any other way they could think of. On New Alexandria, I was as safe as the Library itself, but I didn't want to spend the rest of my life on New Alexandria or on a ferry run to some other repository of human culture at its most arrogant.

I slowly came to realize that circumstances had conspired to make me some immensely powerful and rather nasty-minded enemies. I didn't really see *why* they had to pick on me—I never tried to pick on *them*—but the sinister fact remained. I was free as air, but you'll notice that air has to stick pretty close to its own planet unless it ships out and takes its risks.

All in all, the future did not look rosy.

Still there was no feeler from Charlot, although the news did come back to me via devious means that Jacob Zimmer —one of Charlot's satellites—was looking around for a new crew to take out the *Hooded Swan* as soon as she was released from dry dock. No one sent me any invitations, though.

I knew, however, that everything comes to him who waits (so it's said) and I was prepared to wait, at least until all my money was home again. I spent my days in poverty-stricken idleness debating with Sam the possibility of changing our names and our faces or stowing away on a liner bound for Ultima Thule III. All the while, I was half-expecting something to drift in through the window and make a few insidious suggestions. Rumor had it that Zimmer's vacancy for a pilot remained conspicuously unfilled.

I wasn't disappointed. . . .

"I've been looking for you," he said.

"What a shock," I replied.

"Can I sit down?"

"Please do. You're our first visitor in a very long time. It's not a very nice chair. I'm sorry the room is so crowded, but I'm sharing. I'd introduce you, but I'm afraid he's out just at the moment. Still, you probably know all about him. We couldn't afford the penthouse, you know."

"I hear you're teamed up with a man named Sam Parks," he said, manfully ignoring my sarcasm.

"That's right. He's out looking for work. Downship work. I daresay I might join him. It doesn't seem like a good time to ship out. If we can both get jobs driving cargo trucks or oiling ball-bearings, maybe we need never risk our lives in the desert wastes of deep space ever again. Besides which, Sam has this melodramatic streak in him. Always wanted to be an outlaw. Thinks the Caradoc Company or something similar might hire a gang to snatch us from our beds any night and ship us out to Vargo's Star disguised as a crateful of bananas."

"I see you're keeping well," he said. "What do you think?"

"I gave up thinking," I told him. "It just didn't seem worth it anymore. The load became too much to carry so I just dumped it. At the moment I'm too tired to think. How about you, kid? What sort of thinking are you doing these days? You don't look as well as you reckon I do. Why did they send you, hey? Why didn't they send Eve to seduce me? Or Nick to talk man-to-man? It's too much, of course, to expect that the great man himself would bother to pick me up off the street."

Johnny looked me in the eye, and I realized for the first time that the unnatural stoniness in his face was more than calculated. It wasn't me that was causing it.

"They're dead," he said.

I let a few minutes go by while the residuum of my earlier flippancy was laid completely to rest. The whole atmosphere of the room seemed to change and become heavy and dry. I looked steadily into Johnny's face. It looked older than I remembered it. The image I carried in my mental files for purposes of identification was the image of a teen-age New York shipworker living a slightly sad life above his grandfather's desolate workshops. I hadn't updated my image of Johnny in a year. But I saw him differently now. I saw that he was changed. He looked more like Herault now. He was handsome, and hard.

"What happened?" I asked.

"They took the *Sister Swan* into the Nightingale. They didn't bring it back. Missing, presumed dead. Three of them."

"You didn't go?"

He shook his head. "I didn't go. I wasn't transferred—I'm still the engineer on *your* ship. The *Hooded Swan*. I was hanging about on Darlow like a spare part. No purpose in life except to stand and wait. But they didn't come back."

"You said three," I said. "Who was the engineer?"

"Rothgar." Johnny paused, but I didn't say anything. He shrugged faintly, possibly out of embarrassment. "Charlot picked him up again," he continued. "He was at a dead end. He needed the job. Charlot maybe needed him—thought I couldn't handle the Nightingale. I've not worked space like that . . . not yet. Maybe Charlot was right. Maybe Rothgar couldn't handle the Nightingale either. He . . . wasn't quite the man he might have been. It was catching up with him."

"Bugger you," I said. "Rothgar could handle a piledriver drunk, sick, and senile. Old age would have to move bloody fast to catch up with Rothgar."

"I don't know," he said.

"I do," I told him. I didn't.

"You're trying to make out it was a pilot error," he said. "But you don't know that."

"I'm not trying to make out anything," I told him bitterly. "I don't care whether Eve was a great pilot or not fit to take care of a perambulator. Don't be an idiot." I hoped sincerely that the loss of the *Sister Swan* hadn't brought on a renewal of his old lovesickness. That would be just too much. But he didn't say any more.

I lay back on the bed, trying to figure. It struck me as both horribly inevitable and totally absurd. I'd told them so. Hadn't I told them so? Charlot, I'd said, is *dangerous*.

Not safe, I'd said. He has no regard for our lives. We are expendable. He doesn't care. I'd said it all. Many times. Charlot, I'd said, is asking things no one has any right to ask of human beings. I'd told them so, all right, and they hadn't listened.

And now what?

I felt slightly sick. The sense of loss went right to my belly. It hurt. There wasn't the least vestige of valiant satisfaction at being proved right. There wasn't the least fanfare of relief that it hadn't been me—that I'd got out from under just in time. I was mad at Charlot—bitterly mad—but mostly I just felt like kicking a door down. Some part of me was dead. I didn't love Eve, and I had no respect for Nick, and Rothgar . . . who could have any claim on Rothgar's friendship? But they were all, every one of them, some part of me, and they were squandered. Thrown away into one of the garbage cans of deep space. And why?

Why indeed?

"So what?" I said eventually.

He didn't catch my meaning.

"So what now?" I amplified. "What's the score? Who's winning? Why are you sitting in Sam's chair looking at me like Abraham Lincoln on Mount Rushmore? How come you're the chief supplicant for the Salvation Army cannon-fodder fund? What do you *want?*"

"I came to see you." he said.

"You came to tell me."

"I came to tell you. I was sent back to home base. I found out you were here. I came to see you, to tell you, to talk to you. There's nothing more than that."

"Isn't there?"

"No. Charlot didn't send me. I know what you think, but it's not so. I haven't come to beg you to come out to Darlow."

"Who told you where to find me? Who told you I was even on this world?"

"Denton," he said.

Naturally. Who else?

"Are *you* going back?" I asked him.

"Yes."

"Are you mad?"

"No."

"Eve and Nick and Rothgar are all dead. They took their

ship into the Nightingale and they're dead. And so you naturally come back to little old New Alex and pick up another ship and follow them. That's what Charlot wants, isn't it? Charlot wouldn't admit that he'd got it all wrong, that it's a bum project, that he's a killer and a maniac. Not Charlot. He couldn't. Charlot has to do it a second time, and a third, and a tenth. You don't have to take it, you know. You can tell him to piss off. You can jack it in. You can even commit suicide respectably with a razor blade. But not you. You think you're committed and you haven't the heart to admit that your old friend Grainger had it all right when you had it all wrong. You have to go right ahead, straight down the middle, head low. Why, Johnny, *why?*"

"That's it," he said.

"You can't admit you're wrong?"

"Not that. *Why.* I want to know why. I want to know why that ship didn't come back. I want to know why they died."

"If it kills you too."

"And Charlot."

"Charlot?" For a moment I didn't follow him. Then I saw the light. "Charlot. Of course. He's the guy who can't admit he's wrong. He's not sending out another suicide squad at all—he's going out himself. He's going to prove himself. The only way he knows. The poor fool. It doesn't make any difference, kid. None at all. Don't you see? It's not a matter of cowardice or heroism or integrity. You're not a movie star or a comic book superman. You don't have to be a cretin. It's not obligatory. Don't go, Johnny. Don't fly out with the *Swan*. Leave it alone. Just drop it, and pray that you never clap eyes on Titus Charlot again."

"Why?" he said. "Because I wouldn't be able to look him in the face if I did?"

"Hell, Johnny," I said. "You can't owe anything to a man like that. *You don't have to get killed!*"

"I want to go," he said.

"You're fooling yourself."

"I want to go."

"That's a lie," I insisted. "You're telling yourself lies. You're cheating yourself. What you're trying to do—it isn't being a man, it's being an illusion of a man. There's no point. It's a bummer. A shitout. Hell, I'm *asking* you—don't go."

"What's it to you?" he wanted to know.

What indeed? I understood the question. I could see that he might well be in doubt. Reasonable doubt. When had I ever indicated that I cared?

"I'm sick of counting corpses," I said. "There are too many dead strewn in the corridors of my recent past. Sure, I'm getting old. You expect to see the world age around you. You expect to come into contact with a little death. But this! How many people have you seen die these last few months? How many people have you see close to death? What were you feeling when you were stuck on Mormyr with no pilot and no ship capable of coming down to you? Maybe Alachakh was only an alien to you, maybe you feel the men who died on Pharos had it coming to them . . . but how sick were you? Maybe you don't care about the cops on the *Gray Goose*. But Eve. And Nick. And Rothgar. How high, for God's sake, do you want the pile to grow? So high there's no one left but me to count it? I don't Johnny. I'd like a little bit of the world to stay in one piece. It's comforting to have a bit of the known universe somewhere close at hand. I'd like to know that people still exist—real people, that I've known and touched. That's all, Johnny. I'm sick of counting dead friends. Hell's bells, I don't even want Titus Charlot to die, even if the universe would be better off without him."

He was staring at me. Like Lincoln on Rushmore. A face of stone. I knew I couldn't stop him. There was nothing I could say. He'd been emotionally stranded by tragedy. He cared too much. It wasn't that a youthful passion for Eve Lapthorn had flowered again. It was love of another kind. Not just for Eve. He was cut too deep. He was determined.

"When we were down on Mormyr," he said. "You came to get us. You didn't have to do that. If there was any force to compel you it could only come from inside yourself. You came. It was too dangerous, but you came."

"You're hoping for a rescue," I said. "Is that it? You won't accept that they're dead. You're looking for a miracle. You're looking to *be* a miracle?"

"It doesn't make any difference," he said. "Whether there's a chance or not. Even if we were a hundred percent sure—and how could we be?—I'd want to go."

"To prove somthing."

"Yes."

"Got a pilot?" I asked.

"Not yet."

"Go away, Johnny," I said. "I don't know why, but you're tempting me. I'm too old to make that kind of mistake. Go away."

"OK," he said, making for the door. "Thanks a lot. I'll give your regards to anyone who knows you. Anyone I meet."

He would have walked right out, but just that minute Sam Parks arrived from the port, and they collided in the doorway. The confusion took away all Johnny's impetus, and the old man's eyes threw him right out of his stride. When Sam closed the door, Johnny was still inside.

"Sam," I said, "this is Johnny Socoro."

Sam reached out a hand to grab Johnny's. "They call me Turpin," he said. "But Sam, if you prefer it."

"He knows the joke," I said, before Sam went into his spiel.

"There's a half a dozen liners down," said Sam. "But I can't get near 'em. Nothing doing. Not without a union card. I tried to get a union card. Nothing doing. What kind of world is this?"

He knew what kind of world this was. Who was he trying to kid? He was looking at Johnny pensively.

"He didn't come to offer us a job," I said. "He's just paying us a friendly visit. He came to tell me some news about all my old friends."

"How are they?" asked Sam.

"Dead," I said.

He didn't know where to look. Nor did Johnny. I wanted Sam measuring up the tension in the room. He couldn't figure what was wrong. He knew enough to guess, but not enough to guess right.

"Can we get out of here?" asked Sam. "To somewhere safe?"

"No such place," I said. "Don't raise your hopes on account of Johnny. Mind you, if what he says is true we may be off the hook quite soon."

"How do you mean?" said Johnny.

"If Charlot goes into the Nightingale," I said, "he'll be fixed up for the history books in more ways than one. With Charlot dead, my microscopic role in the game of galactic

bugger-my-neighbor becomes much less important. I'm de-
moted to spear-carrier. Caradoc will forget me. I hope."

They both just looked at me.

"You want some coffee?" said Sam to Johnny.

"No," said Johnny. "I was just going."

"Drop in again," said Sam.

As Johnny was leaving, not quite so stylishly as he had
originally intended, I said to Sam, "Do you remember the
days when we were masters of our own lives? When we
could do what we wanted to without the galaxy persistently
kicking us up the backside? When we were simply toys of
fate?"

"No," he said.

VII

The Nightingale is a weird bird, but not—at first glance —one of the galaxy's most impressive hell-holes.

Most nebulas are ugly and ungainly. They sprawl across the sky in glorious decadent confusion, flaccid and menacing. Nebulas are the wreckage of cosmic disasters, or cosmic disasters in the process of happening, wounds or birthmarks in the fabric of space and time. Their worst dangers lie in their arbitrariness and unpredictability.

The Nightingale is quite different. Perhaps it should not be described as a nebula at all—perhaps a new name should have been invented for it. It's small, as nebulas go, and contains no visible stars. It's shaped like a big lens, and unless you're looking at it edge-on you can see stars through it—blurred and dimmed, but still visible. The space all around the focal lesion is subject to distortive phenomena of the wave-analogue type, but the distortion is oddly regular and possibly predictable. The nebula appears to have a periodic cycle of activity.

So far as I was aware, no one at that time had any idea what the Nightingale might be. I'd never heard any theory to account for it, although no doubt there were a hundred crazy notions with some currency in the space from which the thing was visible. Obviously, Titus Charlot was toying with a hypothesis of his own, trying to come to grips with the enigma and sort it out. I was prepared to admit that if he did manage to find out what went on in the Nightingale it might make a substantial contribution to human understanding of the universe. But I didn't think that was very relevant. Not to me or to the people who were aboard the *Sister Swan*. The fact remained that all nebulas are veritable devils, and he who plays hell with devils is apt to have his hands scorched. Such is life.

I knew full well that I'd have to be a madman to sign back on with the *Hooded Swan* of my own free will, especially after what had happened to the sister ship. The fact that I'd braved the Halcyon Drift and won out didn't really figure. I'd still be dicing with death, and the dice wouldn't be loaded *my* way.

And yet, I was tempted.

I used to think that I know what motives were made of, but it didn't seem so easy just then.

—It never is easy, pointed out the wind, unless you make it easy.

And how do you make it easy? I demanded.

—You decide, he said. And then you make excuses.

You're supposed to find your motives before you make your decisions, I pointed out. Not the other way around.

—Causes, he said, come before effects. But most people start with effects and try to discover causes.

Very glib, I congratulated him. You want to go, don't you? Just like Johnny. Why? Suggest to me some of your excuses. Some of your reasons.

—It's the only game in town, he said. You're wasting your life trying to play a game that ended three years ago. When your ship went down and you buried Lapthorn the final whistle blew on that phase of existence. Ever since then you've been looking backward. Believe me, I know. I know which way's up and it isn't where your head's pointing. You have to start again, but every time you get off the blocks you turn right back in on yourself. The *Hooded Swan* is the game now, and you ought to know that. You of all people know how much of a ship is its pilot and how much of a pilot is his ship. So it's not a bed of roses. So playing this game you have to play by Titus Charlot's rules, which are bent. So OK. All rules are bent. Space is curved. If it wasn't there'd be no such thing as matter. I want to go. All right. I want to go because I don't want to stay here, and neither do you. By "here" I don't mean this room or this world, I mean this head. You're marking time, spinning the present out indefinitely. You still have a future, but every time you begin to move into it you crap out and sag right back. Take the ship. Accept the purpose.

It could kill me.

—Time is killing everybody. Everybody dies.

Great. You talk like a brave man. You always were the

voice of implacable courage and heroism. There's no one big enough so you'll admit he can't be licked. Congratulations. But aren't you forgetting a little something—namely that I die and you don't? When I go, I *go*. You just go to another host.

—I'm not immortal, he said. Nobody lives forever.

But not everybody dies so easily as I do, I told him. You have less to risk and that's all there is to it.

—Maybe, he said, maybe not. But so what? The fact remains. You may have no future if you die, but what does that count for if you're determined to have no future while you live? What are you saving your precious skin *for*, Grainger?

Because I'm fond of it. It hurts me to see it scratched. It's my innate sense of responsibility.

—Fair enough, said the wind. Decide. Stay put. Then ask yourself what your excuses are.

I couldn't just tell him to shut up and push him to the back of my mind. I would have, once. But not forever. Like on Lapthorn's Grave, when the wind begins to talk to you can't ignore him to the end of time. You won't stop the wind blowing. No way.

But I knew my excuses. They were all ready, standing in a row in their Sunday best suits, waiting to be buried. Eve, Nick, Rothgar. All my friends. Alachakh—I sent his coffin into a sun in the Halcyon Drift. Lapthorn—I buried him in a shallow grave on a black mountain. They were all my friends, and they were all my excuses. Going after them wasn't going to help. It was only going to make me one of them. I didn't owe them anything, but if I did it wouldn't be dying. It would be something less dramatic.

But it didn't come easy to me, that decision. Having the excuses all lined up doesn't make it easy. To make it easy, as the wind said, you have to *use* your excuses. And you have to make your decisions first.

I'd be a fool, I thought, to go crawling back to Charlot. A sucker.

—Aren't we all? said the wind.

VIII

But it felt good to be back in the cradle. Really good. It gave me a physical thrill to ease the controls, balancing them in my hands. I felt alive again, healthy after a long sickness of the spirit. I felt as if I were home after an enforced absence. It *had* been enforced.

Tachyonic transfer was a boost into heaven. I felt the power of the flux building up inside me. I felt the wings stretching away from my shoulders. Her vast metal skin was my skin, unblemished. It did more than bring back memories. It brought back identity.

The discovery was a shock. How had I ever let such a feeling sneak out of my mind? I felt as if I'd almost betrayed myself. Then I thought of Johnny and Charlot and the Nightingale, and thought maybe I had.

In tachyonic phase I raced through the hyper-universe, in it and out of it, skimming over its surface but nevertheless supported and contained by it. In turn, I contained a microcosm of my own—a deration field easing gradually as I let her out into the groove. Flux, flowing like blood.

I had to go the long way around in order to make the trip quickly. There were little things in the way like the center of the galaxy. In order to use the *Swan*'s speed I had to go through clean space. All the way in the inner ring. But the long way around was the easy way around. Space is curved anyway. I felt as if I were going with the curve, not against it. Holding the groove put no strain on me. The random factors didn't even threaten to throw me off or rub me the wrong way. It was smooth as silk.

My microcosm was populated by strangers. Johnny, of course, was excluded—an engineer is a part of a pilot's microcosm, not an item in his human cargo. Sam, on the other hand, counted as a stranger. You don't get to know

57

somebody by flying opposite ends of a crate like the *Sandman*. In all the years I rode the *Fire-Eater* and even the *Javelin*, I'd never got to know Lapthorn. Sam was something of an enigma. Still a stranger. I was comfortable when I was with him, but that was all. I thought I might get to know him. He was right down below, sharing the delights of a really first-class mass relaxation drive-unit with Johnny. I'd asked Johnny to let him try his hand with it sometime during the trip. After the things poor Sam had been nursing all his life it would be a sheer joyride. Sam might really fall in love with a heart like the *Swan*'s. He probably never bothered to dream that he'd ever handle anything like it.

The other strangers were people I was never likely to get to know. Sam's presence on the ship was only semi-official. We'd come to Zimmer as a package, and he'd already filled the vacancy for a third crewman. The officer making up the complement was Mina Vogan, a slight, dark-haired girl who'd been riding liners for three years or more. I'd hardly had a chance to speak to her. I could make a guess at the reasons why she'd left the liners for a ship like the *Swan*, but I couldn't help feeling that she was walking blindfold into hell and that Jacob Zimmer—and Charlot, indirectly—were letting her do it. I didn't know what she'd done on the liners—she could have been o-in-c of the catering department or ship's surgeon and still be equally well qualified to take third string on a Library yacht. As her captain, I felt it was my duty to take time out sometime to warn her of the kind of thing she was getting herself into, but I knew she wouldn't let it put her off. What crewman ever takes the ravings of a ship's captain seriously?

We had two passengers. One was Zimmer himself, who had tidied up affairs on New Alex very neatly and was off to lick his master's hand. Zimmer was a nonentity—a relay in the vast human computer which parasitized the real hardware of New Alexandria. He was just an operant function—a flashing light on a display panel. It had been quite straightforward going to him and getting the job. We'd met before, of course, on Hallsthammer, and he'd favored me with a flicker of recognition. Like a true diplomat, he'd not given the slightest sign to indicate that he knew all that had happened between the two meetings. He took me on as pilot and captain without blinking an eyelid. I was momen-

tarily surprised that he handed over the captaincy with a
straight face, when Charlot had taken such care to keep it
out of my hands on past occasions, but I knew that it only
reflected the change in my volunteer status. I was no longer
the rebel, the determined fly in the ointment. I had passed
the test and been made a member of the family. Married to
the Library without a shotgun in my back. Stranger things,
they say, happen in space.

The other passenger was somewhat more important. She
was a doctor. Nobody had told me why she was going to
Darlow, but I had a strong and confident suspicion. Her
name was Lelia Rolfe, and she was a specialist in spinal
diseases. Titus Charlot hadn't been well for some time now,
and I was willing to bet that it wasn't the male menopause
that was bothering him.

Despite the relative overpopulation of my microcosm, I
was alone in the control room for almost the whole duration of the flight. I preferred to celebrate my reunion with
the bird in relative privacy. I didn't want anybody to talk
to me.

I caught the persistent murmur of voices filtering through
the open circuit linking me with the engine room, and I
knew Sam was doing a lot of talking. It had to be Sam because Johnny's mouth would have been close enough to the
mike for me to have heard him if he'd vouchsafed more
than the occasional grunt or monosyllabic reply. I guessed
that Sam was giving him a long chat about his long and
arduous career as a tail-ender or rust-buckets. Johnny could
do worse than listen. There was a lot that Johnny could
learn from Sam if he'd only listen the right way. I could
maybe have taught him the same things myself, but when I
talk in that kind of vein I just don't communicate. I spill
over too much. I haven't Sam's detachment. Sam could explain to him what it was all about without knocking holes
in his head. I hoped Johnny would learn, because Johnny
had a lot in him. He was a potential spaceman—without a
home, or even a race. A man of the transfinite gulf. Provided that he didn't die in the Nightingale.

While the *Swan* grooved at thirty thou for hour after
hour I let my mind run back and forth along a groove of
its own. The man from Caradoc and the farcical way that
Commander Denton of the New Alexandrian Police Force
had snatched me away from his clutching fingers now

seemed like something of a joke. A nonsensical, inconsequential interlude. Soulier had been playing for keeps, playing hard and rough at the game he thought was the *real* man's game. But the whole purpose seemed ludicrous against a background of silent stars. His only interest in me had been commercial. Bribery or vengeance—they were only opposite aspects of the same concern. What was the point? Caradoc's power game had half the known galaxy at stake, but in the final analysis it wasn't actually *for* anything. It wasn't a fight *about* anything. The part I had been cut out to play was so monumentally trivial as to be quite absurd. A joke of truly minuscule proportions.

My mind had to go back through Soulier to Nick delArco before I discovered anything worth thinking about. *Captain* delArco. I couldn't quite work out how long it had been since I pulled him out of that storm on Mormyr. And what for? So he could commit suicide in a dark nebula. The score might be level between me and fate, because Johnny was still alive. One apiece. But even so it was annoying to think that so little had been gained by saving Nick's worthless hide. Poor Nick. A sucker all along the line. A prince of suckers. His mother had no right to turn him out of his playpen with so little preparation for the wicked wide world and its evil ways. A good guy, Nick. A *nice* guy.

I knew I could forget Nick, but I knew I wouldn't. Somehow, he had contrived to leave an impression. Eve was different. Eve I couldn't forget even if I wanted to. She'd echoed in my mind just a little too loud. She'd echoed Lapthorn, and I could no longer think Lapthorn without knowing that there were two of them. Brother and sister. Man and ghost. I couldn't count the number of times my reaction-pattern to Lapthorn had taken hold of my behavior toward Eve. She might have interpreted that as an endless series of small cruelties. She could hardly understand. I'd never tried to explain. She could have died hating me. And all for nothing. All for a fake relationship. I hadn't loved Eve. Not ever. But I just might have, perhaps, if it hadn't been for the Lapthorn reactions that had got into me.

You did all this to me, I accused the wind. You've turned my head around. If it wasn't for you . . . why the hell should I feel *guilty?* Was it me who killed them?

—No, he said.

IX

We made level time to Darlow. There was plenty of time for things to happen, but nothing did. The *Swan* was in perfect shape. All the pounding she'd taken in the Leucifer system had left not a mark on her. They'd done a good job back on New Alexandria. She was her old self, in every detail. If it were mechanically and humanly possible to make the flight that Charlot had planned, then the *Swan* and I were fit for it. The only question mark was Johnny.

Darlow was a desolate ball of impure iron whose only conceivably useful feature was its closeness to the Nightingale Nebula. It was a small planet of a tired rose-colored sun. Its air wasn't poisonous but it contained very little oxygen and life of our kind could only be supported courtesy of abundant artificial aid. The planet wasn't inhabited, in the normal sense of the word, but New Alexandria had maintained a dome there for a long time, partly as an element in the vast web of New Alexandria interests which threaded the known galaxy, and partly for the specific purpose of observing the enigmatic Nightingale. The base never supported anything resembling a thriving community, but its population tended to be fairly stable; there were men and women who spent all their working lives there, and a handful of children had been born there. Technically, therefore, it counted as one of the vast number of "human" worlds, and like Earth or Penaflor it added no less and no more than one to the numerical total. On statistics like that the success of the human race is measured. People will claim we are the galaxy's primary inhabitants because we "possess" more worlds than the Khor-monsa, the Gallacellans, and all the rest put together. People do say it. All the time.

The people who lived their lives here spent the time in

between ships digging holes in the ground looking for
whatever they might find or writing the great Darlovian
novel. Many of them had a fierce patriotism. It had to be
fierce, because there was no other way to answer the questions put to it. The transients—mostly peripatetic technical
staff theoretically based on New Alexandria (though they
might never see "home" in their entire lives) were forced
to acquire a shadow of the same patriotism. They couldn't
live without it. The spacemen who used Darlow as a stop-
over or a communication point had to respect the idiosyncrasies of the people. You insult the honor of Darlow at
your peril. Pride is a dangerous thing not to have, or at
least to know about, on a world like that.

Somehow, I couldn't help thinking that Abram Adams—
the senior man on the base and virtually the world's dicta-
tor—was something other than human. I could see hardly
anything that we held in common except a shape and a
language. And the Khor-monsa always speak better English
than most grounders. The smaller a world the faster it gains
and loses words from its pooled vocabulary. The only standard tongue in this day and age is the spacer tongue.

The dome was no more than a mile across and it wasn't
exactly high-density living inside. People on little worlds
like lots of personal space. New Alexandria was prepared
to cater to that, uneconomic or not. Tragedies had been
known to happen in domes in the early days, and still did
sometimes. This meant that we were each assigned quarters
considerably more salubrious than a starship cabin, and
apparently quite luxurious for such a poor world. My rooms
included a sitting room whose north wall was a great curved
window, commanding a fine view of the bubble-city. The re-
fractive effect of the dome, a plastic interface between gases
of different density and makeup, tended to blur the aspect
of the land outside the dome, refusing to admit to the sharp-
ness and bleakness of the landscape, but making it strange
and mysterious.

I couldn't stay long in my quarters to enjoy the view—
not that I enjoyed it much anyway—because a captain has
duties to perform. A mere pilot can crawl into his shell
when his ship touches down, but a captain is always a
captain. I had to see the port authority, and Adams himself,
and last—but hardly least—I had to see Charlot. I changed
my clothes, and brushed my recently cut hair, and then I

sallied forth, with the habitual puposeful stride of the man
with responsibilities.

I cut it all short, not because I was in a hurry to get to
Charlot, but because I found it all mildly distasteful.

Circumstances rushed me to the inevitable confronta-
tion. I let them.

He was waiting for me.

His face was deadpan, but I thought I could sense a trace
of satisfaction—and a hint of pain—in the way he looked
at me. He was seated, and he didn't get up to greet me. I
think the pain might have shown clearly had he attempted
to rise. There was a lamp on the desk in front of him, which
he was using in preference to the light set in the ceiling. The
top half of his face was in shadow, all except for his eyes,
which caught the light and glistened.

The room was bare and the heating was turned up pretty
high. I sat down opposite him, and as he moved forward
to bring himself closer to me I saw the strain in the way he
supported himself, and the deadness in the way his weight
hung about the cushioned chair. The gravity on Darlow was
less than two-thirds par, and I felt distinctly buoyant. But
he'd been here for some time.

"Hello, Grainger," he said. His voice was cool and collected.

"Mr. Charlot," I acknowledged, nodding my head
slightly.

"I wasn't sure that I was going to see you again," he said.

"I was sure," I told him, "but I was wrong."

"It doesn't do to be too sure," he commented. "Things
happen. Things change. One can't always see the reasons
for tomorrow's actions.

"Or today's," I added.

A shadow crossed his face. "Tell me about the incident
on Erica."

"There's not much to tell. The Caradoc Company apparently took note of the fact that Fate had allowed you and
I to drift apart. They took a keen interest. They don't like
me, and they have a pathological hatred of you and yours.
They seemed to feel an urgency to step into the breach between us. They wanted to buy all that I knew about you.
You know what that might be worth better than I—or they
—possibly could. I don't think they'd have got much out of
me that would repay their trouble, and I didn't want to

make a deal anyhow. But they seemed anxious to make me an offer I couldn't refuse. There was only one of them, actually—do you know a man called Soulier?—but I felt outnumbered. Heavily. I tried to get out of sight, but he planted something on me while I wasn't looking. I was in the net, but the law snatched me out. Your law."

Charlot looked dour.

"I'm truly sorry about that," he said. "I didn't anticipate it. Perhaps I should have."

"You've been getting in their hair rather a lot," I pointed out.

He shook his head. "I stand for New Alexandria," he said. "I think they have already declared war, in their minds, against New Alexandria. This was not the first blow, and there will be many more before hostilities move out into the open. Most of their enemies, they can fight— they can apply leverage and use force. Against New Alexandria, they need something different. They are thrashing about blindly, catching loose ends, hoping. It will get worse, not better."

"I don't want to be on the battlefield," I said. "It's not my fight. You know that I don't take sides."

"The people who don't take sides," said Charlot, "will *become* the battleground. That's what the fight is all about. Believe me, Grainger, when I say that I am sorry. You are involved, perhaps against your will. I accept the blame for that. Perhaps you should remember, though, that the whole human race is involved. It is your future, and the future of every other man, that is being decided by the actions and counteractions of the companies and the humanitarian worlds."

"Crap," I said.

He didn't flinch.

"I'm glad you came back with the *Hooded Swan*," he said. "I think I need you now."

"Maybe so," I said. "But you'll forgive me if I save my gratitude until I know exactly what you need me *for*. You want someone to take the ship into that nebula. I'm here. Not because of you, or because of whatever you hope to achieve, but I'm here."

"I'm grateful to you," he said.

"Look," I replied. "You know and I know that at best

we dislike one another and at worst we despise one another. Let's not be hypocrites. Just tell me the plan."

He stared at me, a curious expression on his face that I could not identify.

"I don't despise you," he said.

"Great," I said. "Let's not argue about it."

He nodded slowly, his eyes drifting down to the assortment of paper on his desk. Most of it was computer output, but there were some scribbled notes and a few pages of apparently flimsy reports attached to data collations.

"It isn't a matter of going into the nebula," he said. "Far from it. The idea is to go through it."

"To go through it," I pointed out, "you have to go into it."

"You don't understand," he said. "The nebula is an interface. A boundary between spaces. The *Swan* will go into the lens from this space, but it will emerge into another. Another universe."

I leaned back, balancing my hands lightly on the plastic arms of the chair, drumming my fingers softly on the extremities. I still felt oddly light because of the low gee, but my heart had accelerated, and my gut seemed to be moving."

"That's where the other ship went," I said. "They were *trying* to blast their way clean out of the universe. And they did it. But they didn't come back. And you're surprised? Why? Who expects to come back from nowhere? Who can possibly expect to come back?"

I remembered the way the *Swan* and I—and Nick and Eve and Rothgar—had exited from the contortive domain in the Drift when the *De Lancy* and her little friends had fired a clutch of missiles at us. We'd gone through a hole. Nick and Eve had been blissfully unaware—what had Rothgar known? I remembered what I thought then . . . the way I felt when, just for an instant, I didn't know whether I'd come through. I could have ended up in another time, another space, or strewn all over the continuum. In that second, I'd been halfway to nowhere and if I hadn't been drugged up to the eyeballs and wind infested I'd have been out of my tiny mind with fear.

I'm a spaceman. I like emptiness and darkness. But space isn't nowhere—it's *here*. Space is where we *all* live—the matrix of existence. Charlot really wanted to pull off the

big one this time. The grandest of all his coups—his swan
song? One universe wasn't big enough to remember Charlot. He wanted two. Maybe he wanted them all. A man
who never saw a hole without poking his finger into it. Or
somebody else's finger.

"I'll explain it to you," he said.

"You do that," I replied. "And better make it good. Because it sounds to me like murder."

"Do you know what the Nightingale is?"

"As well as anybody, except you."

"Do you know why they call it the Nightingale?"

I didn't. "Because it sings?" I suggested.

"In a way. We've observed stars through the nebula for
years. It looked like a lens and it was only natural to treat
it like one. From what we knew of the stars we were looking at and by studying the light that actually came out of
the nebula we thought we could find out a great deal about
nebular behavior. We did. We found out a very great deal
about the behavior of *this* nebula. We didn't solve any of
the mysteries of the universe, because what goes on here
is something altogether special, but we did find somthing
most interesting.

"Some of the light which goes into the nebula never
comes out. We thought for a long time that none did—that
the radiation emitted was wholly independent of that observed. But that's not so. The stars that are seen in the lens
are the stars beyond it. It's just that their radiation suffers
a considerable depletion *somewhere* in or beyond the lens.

"The emissive behavior of the nebula is striking. Extremely regular. It follows a distinct periodic pattern, not
just in quantity of emission, but in the composition of the
radiation emitted. It's not detectable, except with sophisticated instruments, of course, but it can be made available
for direct sensory appreciation by translating electromag-
netic impulses into sounds. Some of the observers here, just
for the hell of it, orchestrated the pattern. It plays quite a
lovely tune. The absolute constancy of the pattern can be
detected quite easily by ear—the ear, of course, is much
more sensitive to variations of frequency and quality of
sound than the eye is to small changes in light. That's how
the nebula came to be known as the Nightingale."

"Very interesting," I commented dryly.

"The most interesting observation is that the nebula is

causing our universe a net loss of energy," said Charlot. "The radiation doesn't all come back and there is nothing —absolutely *nothing*—in our observations to account for the residuum. We have a very good idea indeed of the anatomy of the lesion. We have the pattern of contortion defined perfectly. We have a mathematical model of the nebula which works—*if* we provide it with an alternative continuum into which it can leak its energy. There's another universe which 'touches' ours at the Nightingale, and ours is bleeding into it—bleeding energy.

"I think that it's possible to reach that other universe. In fact, I'm sure of it. If the *Sister Swan* proved nothing else she surely proved that. It's possible to pass through the lens from one space to the other."

"If you say so," I told him, "I believe you. I believe that's where the *Sister Swan* went to, and I know that whatever the *Sister Swan* can do the *Hooded Swan* can duplicate. But the important question seems to me to have been overlooked. It may be possible to go into this other universe all right—but is it possible to come back?"

"I hope so," he said.

"You hope so. On the basis of hope you sent Eve Lapthorn, Nick delArco, and Rothgar into the nebula. Now, armed with no more than the same hope—which by now must be somewhat more slender—you expect me to try. You want to risk another ship, and more people. How many? Me, Johnny, Mina Vogan? Passengers? Maybe you, maybe the doctor? Who else?"

"Nobody else," he said.

"You can't do it," I told him. "You mustn't be allowed to do it. Three is too many to die for a crazy idea like this one. Hope is just *not enough*, Titus. Not mathematical modeling, not a mountain of observation, and not all the theorizing acumen tucked away in your little skull. I'm the captain of the *Hooded Swan* this trip, Mr. Charlot, and I have legal responsibility. I can take a decision. And I won't waste Johnny, or the girl, or the doctor, or even you and me. It's not on."

And he smiled.

I knew then that he wasn't making any mistakes. He knew me. He knew me, maybe, better than I did. He'd been expecting this.

"I didn't think I needed you," he said. "On the surface, it

didn't appear that expert piloting would be required. A certain delicacy, but more demanding from the engineer's point of view than the pilot's. The ship, you see, goes in along the axis. A perfect groove. The distance involved need not be large—the computer can handle everything this side of the lens. It's necessary that the crossover should take place as near cee as possible—as you're aware, of course, the existential status of an MR ship in tachyonic phase is somewhat dubious, and I'm not sure that it would work at transcee. Subcee is, of course, much safer from everyone's point of view. That's where the engineer has problems, of course, keeping everything in balance close to the Einstein barrier. I had every confidence that Johnny Socoro would be able to cope, but I was unhappy about his mental state following your departure. I thought it altogether wiser to substitute Rothgar."

"If you've got a point," I said, "come to it."

"The point is this," he said. "I think I do need you. I think that it *was* pilot error that resulted in the *Sister Swan's* failure to return. I think the ship went through perfectly—and then something happened on the other side."

"Attacked by Apaches?" I suggested.

"Something went wrong," he continued, ignoring my fatuous remark. "I think that you can handle it, knowing that something may be liable to happen. I have perfect confidence in Johnny, provided that you're with him. I have every confidence in you. I'm coming with you, to prove it."

He still had his ace in the hole, and he was in no hurry to play it. But I could already guess what it might be. The only way to make a man stick his head in a mousetrap is to bait it. I knew what was coming. But I let him go on.

"We know the ship got through to the other side," he said. "The energy-metabolism of the nebula hasn't altered, as it would have if the *Sister Swan* was destroyed or time-slipped. And there's something else. Something I want you to listen to."

He pushed back from the desk. The chair moved away on castors, and he swiveled to face the wall. There was a stereophonic deck there, with a cassette all ready to play. He switched it on and turned up the volume.

"This," he said, "is the song of the Nightingale, recorded some months ago at a point along the axis of the lens."

A sequence of notes, meaningless but quite pretty, poured from the speakers. I soon picked out the pattern that was repeating. Charlot let it go on for several minutes, through three or four full periods, and then switched off. He removed the cassette and pulled another one from the slot below the deck. He shoved it into place and switched on again. Then he spun his chair through half a revolution and looked at me.

"This is what it sounds like now," he said.

The words mingled with the cadences. He let it play through several times again. I couldn't really pin down the difference, but I knew there had to be one. There had to be something new in the pattern that was coming out now. It hadn't spoiled the song, so far as I can tell. But I'm damn near tone deaf.

"So what?" I said.

"That's the *Sister Swan*."

"Is that a fact?"

"The nebula hasn't changed its pattern in all the years we've been monitoring it," he said. "Until the *Sister Swan* went through. We knew what kind of radiation came out of the nebula and we set up the ship's emergency bleep to comply with that. We wanted to know, you see—to be sure."

"You can't be sure," I said. "You don't know that's the bleep. The ship could have blown up. *Something* would come back out, whatever had happened. Naturally, that something would be in the permissible range. You can't know that it's a bleep."

"It's *regular*," said Charlot, knowing he was on a winner. "It's consistent. It has a pattern. It fits in with the tune. That's not the result of an explosion. It's the bleep, Grainger. I designed that signal. I recognize it. The ship is still whole. It's still functioning."

"You're trying to tell me they're alive," I said.

"Yes."

"And if I believe you," I said, "you think that makes it all OK?"

"Yes."

"Johnny didn't say a word about the possibility of their being alive," I said. "Not one word."

"Johnny doesn't know," he said.

"Why not?"

"Because he doesn't need to know. I want him the way he is now. Cold as ice. I don't want to turn him into a tear-away hero."

He stopped as though he were stopping short, leaving something unsaid.

"And . . . " I prompted.

"I wanted you back before you knew. I wanted you to take the job on the *Swan* because it was there, not because *you* felt like playing hero."

"I don't see that that makes any difference," I said.

"I do," he told me. "It puts things square. It puts us on an honest basis. That twenty thousand you had to pay off . . . that put pressure on you. Too much pressure. I wanted the pressure off. I wanted you working for me without strings. You're the captain now, and you have the responsibility. You can say no. They're your decisions now."

I was somewhat taken aback. "You're trying to con me," I said.

"No," he said, "I'm not. You're an intelligent man, Grainger, and a capable one. I don't want to fight you. In the past . . . well, what happened in the past is over. I think we can play the same game now. On the same side."

I wasn't sure that I was hearing right. Here was Titus Charlot promoting me from puppet back to human being. For what? Not because he wanted me to ride the *Swan* into the nebula. Not just for that. Because I'd helped him on Pharos? Or because he'd sat on my back too long and too hard in the Leucifer system? I couldn't even make a guess. Maybe it was a deathbed repentance of all his wicked ways.

"They might not be alive," I said, changing the subject back to something I *did* understand.

"They might not," he agreed.

"I take it they can't get a call out?"

He shook his head. I shrugged.

"Fair enough," I said. "When do we start?"

"You've changed your mind?"

I looked sharply at him. "Not because of what you've just said," I told him. "I'm not going for the soft soap. I wouldn't have come out here unless I'd meant to get in on the action. If there's a possibility they're all right, I'll see what I can do. That's all."

"There's one more thing you ought to know," he said.

"What's that?"

"The bleep. I said that I recognized it. I do. But it took some time. There's something wrong with it. There's something wrong with the period. The other continuum may be distorted relative to ours—not just at the interface but throughout . . . it may be stranger that we can possibly expect."

I let a few moments pass in silence. Then I said, "I don't see any point in risking more than we have to. I want the girl to stay here. And I think you should stay as well."

"No," he said.

"It's too dangerous," I insisted. "With Sam along, we don't need the girl. We don't need your doctor, and we don't need you. We could do it with two, three is crowded. You're a sick man. You'd be more of a liability than a help."

His face flared. He came upright in his chair and I saw the pain in the wrinkles around his eyes. His jaw was set firm. He was angry, bitterly angry, in a way that I'd never seen before. He was usually the coldest of men, with never more than an edge to his temper. But now he was inflamed. I'd touched something very sensitive. Not his sickness . . . his uselessness. He couldn't and wouldn't face that.

"You need me," he said. "If something unforeseen does happen. If the alternate continuum *is* alien . . . beyond what we normally understand by the word. We can't take undue risks . . . that's your philosophy, isn't it? Don't you think sending out an undercrewed ship is a risk? Don't you think that leaving behind the best mind at your disposal is a risk? This isn't a joyride and I'm not going for the pleasure of it. I'm going because I want to *know* what went wrong. I want to *know* what's on the other side of that doorway. I'm going to die soon, and you know that as well as I do. I'll never go home again, and perhaps you've guessed that too. From here I have nowhere to go except an orbital satellite. I can't take one gee . . . not ever again. From this moment on, Grainger, the *Hooded Swan* is going to be my home for at least half the time that remains to me. If I can get the alterations done here I'm going to have a gee-canceled environment set up in some of the cabins. The doctor is going to be with me forever. I need the spare crewman too. You may not think that it's important for us to be on the same side, but I do. From now on, we all act as a team. You, me, the ship, and all who ride in her. Do you understand?"

I nodded. And now, I think, I did understand. I saw what it meant to him. He'd never see New Alex again. What time was left to him, he wanted to spend productively. The inner compulsion which drove him into problem after problem—intellectual and social and historical—wasn't going to let up because of a little thing like impending death. Titus Charlot was about to become a spaceman, because he had no other choice. His body would not support him in a gravity well. The *Hooded Swan* was his life, now—or would be soon. I hadn't been recovered for one little mission—not simply to face one more set of dangers. I wasn't to be Titus Charlot's puppet anymore. I was going to be his crutch.

I hated the idea.

Without even knowing why, I recoiled from the thought. I thought of deep space and flying as freedom. No matter who else was aboard my ship, it always remained *my* ship. But what Charlot was suggesting added a new factor to all that. Titus wanted to make the ship—*and me*—a shell to protect his soft little body. As if he were a mollusk or a turtle . . . as if he were a hermit crab dispossessing a whelk.

"No," I said.

"I'm not offering you any choices," said Charlot. "That's the way it's going to be. That's the job. You know I'm right, in any case. I sent the ship out with a skeleton crew before, and look what happened. This is a foray into the absolute unknown. You must realize that. There's no question of going without me. Whatever we have to cope with beyond the nebula . . . you need me."

I daren't contradict him. Not again. For the moment, I was up against the wall.

"You'd better sleep now," said Charlot. "There's work to be done on board ship. The computers have to be programmed. We'll lift as soon as possible—after everyone is thoroughly briefed about what we're doing. The only thing that we keep quiet is the possibility that the others may be alive. Understood?"

"Titus," I said quietly. "Did it ever occur to you that you might be mad?"

"I'm not mad," he told me.

I'd had varying opinions about the matter in the past. I still wasn't sure. But I sure as hell didn't like the way things were. Not at all.

I went away, to sleep on it.

X

Charlot's timetable left me with a little time to spare the next day. I was grateful for that, at least. It gave me time to try to weigh up the situation.

I knew there was no point in tackling Leila Rolfe on the matter of Charlot's health, but there had to be a resident medic who'd be as familiar with the case as anybody. Like everyone else who spent a great deal of time here he was other things as well as a doctor, but that didn't make him any less one. He didn't want to talk either, but I threw him a line about my taking responsibility for Charlot's life out in space, and how I couldn't do it without knowing the full facts from an informed and unbiased viewpoint. I demanded to know the truth, the whole truth, and nothing but the truth about Charlot's sad and sorry state, and he gave it to me.

It was bad.

Too bad to be participating in crazy exploits like the one I was about to undertake. At best, the doctor pointed out, the mission would be very taxing, and at worst extremely hazardous. And whatever *my* chances of getting out alive might be—on which subject he wasn't qualified to express an opinion, but he wasn't going to put any money on it—Charlot's could be reckoned as virtually nil. What's more, said the doctor, Charlot knew that.

I wasn't so sure. Titus Charlot might have been *told* that he was on the losing end of the game, but getting him to take what he was told could be a very different matter.

The medic had a word of advice to offer me.

"Don't go," he said. "The old man is in a tearing hurry. You can understand that. But in that tearing hurry he's trying to beat the clock, which just can't be done. This whole thing has been set up in a flat rush. It's crazy. He's been jumping conclusions right, left, and center. He's a brilliant man, but not while he's this way. It may be OK for him . . . what has he got to lose? But for you, and your crew . . .

"We can sort out this thing, given time, and care, and sanity. We'll solve the problems of the Nightingale—we can send out probes and bring them back. We can do the job as it should be done—slowly. This crazy rush to waste ships and men . . . it's inhuman."

I thanked him kindly, and went on my way. Privately, I only half-agreed with him. Crazy it all might be, but inhuman . . . no.

With an hour or two to spare before the lift, I went right up to the top of the dome to the observation tower. It was deserted except for a couple of automated tracking devices. Most of the so-called observation which went on at the base was conducted by far more devious means than looking out of the window.

It was evening, local time, and Darlow's cold red sun was hovering like a forlorn balloon over the jagged horizon. The sky was already draped with a blue-black night in the east, and the stars of the core were clearly visible. The thin atmosphere didn't catch and scatter the sunlight to any great degree, but the color change across the arch of the sky was nevertheless dramatic.

The landscape itself was harsh and broken, but oddly reflective. The hacked-up, cratered surface which stretched away for a mile or so and then ended abruptly in a close skyline seemed almost polished in the way it gleamed silver and pink. The planet reminded me somewhat of a crushed car, all squashed into a ball ready for feeding back into the plant for recycling. A scrap-metal planet.

The Nightingale was clearly visible in the northeast. It looked nothing like a bird—but then, neither did the Halcyon Drift. Apart from the idiosyncrasies of their nomenclature the two had almost nothing in common. The Halcyon, as seen in the skies of nearby worlds, sometimes used to remind me of a witch's caldron in which all kinds of filthy brew was on the boil. Its shape, if it could be said to have a shape, was reminiscent of a spider or a feather-star. A great clutching hand, Eve had called it, when we were on Hallsthammer. Maybe from a very long way off an imaginative onlooker might have compared it to a kingfisher, but close up it was all hate and fury.

The Nightingale was altogether different. From Darlow, it was oval, because we were thirty degrees or so aslant from the axis of the lens. It was set against a thin field of stars, and might have occluded as many as six or eight that would be visible to the naked eye here. Its apparent diameter—the length of the long axis from my point of view—was a good deal greater than that of the sinking sun. It was like a pit in the sky—a silver-gray rim fading to utter blackness at the center. The whole body was surrounded by a faint halo of blue light, but I think that was an optical illusion rather than a cosmic phenomenon. From Darlow, it looked more like a concave lens than a convex one. It wasn't hard to imagine it as a hole in a silver ring. Perhaps not so much a doorway as a perforated ulcer. An open wound in the gut of the universe. Looking at it, I felt as if my line of sight were being *drawn* toward the center, tracking from silver to black, searching for the heart of ultra-blackness that could never be quite there.

While I was looking at it and thinking about it Sam Parks looked in. He was obviously looking for me, because he promptly threw the door open and entered.

"Don't tell me," I said. "My absence has been noted and they want me back on duty forthwith, if not sooner."

He shook his head.

"Other way around," he said. "Lift's been put back. Tomorrow morning, now."

"Why?"

He shrugged. "I don't know. Computer's fed. All operational. If I was to guess, I'd say the old man doesn't feel too good. He's been moving around a good deal, and it doesn't look like moving around suits him any too well."

"If there's no reason given," I said, "that's what it'll be. I wonder if I might talk him out of it if I catch him with a pain in his back . . . ?"

I gave up that particular line in wondering very quickly. Charlot in pain was liable to be just as inflexible as Charlot in the pink, only twice as nasty.

Sam was looking at the nebula. He eased himself forward to lean on the rail and press his face right up to the transparent wall of the dome.

"Doesn't seem like such a good idea anymore, hey?" I said gently.

"Maybe not," he said. He didn't sound too unhappy, but all the excitement had left him.

"Not really your thing at all," I said. "Intrepid rush into danger. Old man on brink of death. Mock-heroic space pilot and aging crony. Youngster in the engine room. Seemingly impossible rescue attempt set against a background of cosmic concepts sufficient to make the mind boggle. Isn't quite what it was in *Planet Stories,* though, is it?"

"Pretty much," he said. "It's only a bit less comfortable."

I felt a slight twinge of conscience about using the word "rescue" when I wasn't supposed to be mentioning the fact that they might be alive, but Sam hadn't taken it seriously.

"Comfortable?" I said. "Hell, I'll lay odds Dick Turpin got saddle-sore riding to York."

"Dick Turpin never rode to York," said Sam. "He just galloped up the great north road a way, yelling 'I'm going to York'—then he hid in Sherwood Forest till the heat was off, went back home, and said he'd been and come back again. You know how gullible people are."

"Sure," I said. I wasn't quite certain how Sherwood Forest got into the wrong myth, but I wasn't in any position to call him a liar.

There was a long pause, while he contemplated the sky and I contemplated him.

"If we were sane," I said, eventually, "and Titus Charlot was sane, we would never have got into this mess in the first place. But that's not the way the world goes, is it? Just because we're reasonable men doesn't mean that we're disbarred from acting like idiot kids. If you'd asked me, two years ago, when I was on a lump of rock with certain vague similarities to this one with every prospect of staying there for the rest of my unnatural life, what I could conceivably be doing at the heart of a tangled web of lunacy like this, I would have laughed at you. I wouldn't have been able to see it at all. No way. But here I am. Mock hero—maybe about to turn mock turtle. Am I downhearted? Yes. Am I chickening out? No. Why not? Well . . . "

"Give it a rest," he said soberly.

I gave it a rest.

"I think you're right," he said, after a moment.

"What?"

"We're not disbarred. We're entitled."

"You don't want to back out?"

"Hell," he said, "no."

It was later—much later—that I really began to make the figures add up in the balance sheets of my mind. If the lift hadn't been put back . . . maybe if I hadn't had that little crosstalk with Sam . . . I probably wouldn't have got my head on straight at all. But he who needs to hesitate often finds hesitation thrown his way.

I knew the score. I was the only one who did, because only Charlot knew about the bleep and he was disqualified because he couldn't add. Not realities—only numbers.

I tried to get some sleep before the lift, though I wasn't tired—it seemed to have been a short day, even though we were reckoning standard and not local. Instead of sleep, I found myself with a real attack of racing trepidation. I lay down on my bed and I closed my eyes, and the ideas marched out of my hind-brain in battalions.

I hadn't taken a sleeping pill. Normally, I didn't need them. I always prided myself on coolness and take-it-as-it-comes.

The fear struck into me like a barbed arrow.

Suppose, I thought . . . just suppose . . . that there's nothing on the other side of that hole in the sky but a great big hunger that ate the *Sister Swan* and is going to eat me. Suppose that new note in the song is nothing but bait.

They'd have to rename the nebula "The Siren."

I could visualize the nebula, just then, not as an ulcer but a grinning, gaping mouth with silvery lips fading into an abyssal black gullet.

I realized that I'd already been eaten away by that mouth. It had already chewed up a part of my life in consuming Eve Lapthorn and Nick delArco and Rothgar. Another greedy multi-jawed cosmic maw had swallowed up the *Javelin* and Michael Lapthorn and Alachakh and Cuvio. A lot of my past had been digested by the Halcyon Drift. Chewed, churned, and assimilated.

What was left of me?

Or, to be strictly accurate, what would be left of me after I'd offered the rest of my life to be devoured by the Nightingale? A sacrifice to a voracious idol. On a silver plate: Johnny Socoro, all that remained of Herault and

Earth and New York Port and the repair shop, and the shadows of my youth; Titus Charlot, the man who had been the architect of the last year of my life; the *Hooded Swan*, flesh of my flesh, the being whose soul I was.

And me. All of the essential me. On the same silver plate.

Even the wind. . . .

I added all these things together. I added Sam Parks and a girl who passed for extra crew, and a doctor who might have greater things to do than put Charlot together when his eggshell shattered. They were just seasoning—delegates from the human race to an adventure into futility. Only the human race—the thread in the fabric of my life.

It all made a handsome parcel. Well over the limit. It couldn't be done.

Lapthorn said I had no soul, and he was right, but I could add two and two and make two too many.

Titus Charlot had his place in the history books. New Alexandria would erect a statue to his memory, and engrave his obituary on cold steel to last forever. Almost.

Eve Lapthorn had parents back in . . . was it Illinois? . . . who probably hadn't added a single wrinkle or passed a single thought since I'd sat in their drawing room and told them their son was dead.

But what about Nick, or Sam, or Johnny? Or me?

The wind was somewhere inside me, lost and quiescent. He never said a word. He was there, all right, in spirit. He didn't have to interfere anymore. We'd achieved harmony. The symbiosis that had always been his aim and his claim. We were in it together—in the thinking and the hesitating and the decision-taking. A silent consipracy. We were dreaming a communal dream.

I *was* dreaming, though I wasn't asleep. I could see it all inside my head. In technicolor. One nightmare, medium rare.

I didn't go to sleep. Instead, I got up and I got dressed. I washed my face to make myself feel cool and alive. Then I went out into the corridor, and sneaked along on tiptoe until I found Sam's room. I went in and I crouched beside the bed. I put my hand over his mouth while I woke him up. I was very quiet—I held my breath a long time and released it slowly and carefully, and then sucked it in again just the same way.

I stopped him saying anything, and I whispered in his ear.

"Come on, Turpin," I said. "This is your big moment in life. We're going to hijack a starship."

XI

I wouldn't let him say a word. All the way down to the airlock we were absolutely silent. It was dead easy to rip off two suits and disappear through the lock into the darkness before the dawn. Nobody expects thieves on a world like Darlow. Anyone who wants to prowl at night is one hundred percent welcome. Nothing is guarded, no doors are locked. There was no one to challenge us in or out of the dome.

It was only a five-minute walk out to the ship. We set out in darkness, but by the time we got there the sun was already hoisting itself above the horizon. It didn't matter. There was no one to see us.

Once inside the *Swan* we stripped off rapidly. Again, he tried to talk, to find out what the hell I was about, but again I wouldn't let him. I didn't want to waste any time explaining, and I certainly didn't want to begin and then discover that I didn't *have* an explanation. I was riding an impulse and I wasn't about to let anything get in its way. I shoved him bodily along the corridor into the engine room, and I started up the ladder to the control room.

Once we had a nice, impersonal call-circuit in between us, I was willing to exchange a few words. But strictly business.

"Now look, Sam," I said, when I was settled into the cradle. "Count me down nice and easy. But when we let those cannons go we are going to *go*. Up and away. I don't want any damned fool running out of the lock in a light suit and getting blinded by our backburn. We haven't much area to spare on the ground. I want a quick, tight lift. OK?"

"Grainger," he said. "What are we doing?"

"Never mind the chatter," I said. "Start the countdown."

81

The countdown began. As we began to feed power into
the piledriver we started making noise. Not much, but
enough to wake a light sleeper despite the thinness of the
air and the thickness of the dome. On a world like Darlow
people get used to silence, and anything that isn't is apt
to disturb them. I hoped no one would react until the
cannons let go. Then the vibrations transmitted through
the ground would have them out of their beds in a hurry,
but by then it would be too late even to ask us what was
going on.

The countdown went into the tens and nobody showed.
I knew we were away, then. At zero the cannons began
to burn. The reaction in the thrust chamber swelled quickly
but smoothly, and we began to haul ourselves from the
ground almost immediately, riding the cushion of the blast.
Impulse from the discharge points flooded the deration
system and the flux was urged into action. Sam kept the
syndrome under control—he didn't stifle it, but there was
never a chance of its running wild.

We lifted with majestic perfection.

Power surged through the nerve-net and brought my
ship-self vibrantly alive. I felt the span and the sweep of
the wings.

We were clear of the atmosphere in no time at all.

"Countdown to tachyonic transfer," I said levelly.

"Check," said Sam, and began in the two-twenties. He
was being conservative—understandably. I didn't want
him to rush. We had all the time in the world now. There
was nothing that could stop us. We were free and clear.

The call-circuit burped slightly, and I closed down the
outside tap. I wanted only the control-to-drive relay. The
rest was spare. It was illegal to cut out the circuit like that,
but I'd already broken enough laws for a few more to
make no difference. Captains have authority, but not the
kind of authority I'd taken upon myself.

I felt the relaxation field growing. Sam was balancing
it carefully, taking no chances at all, feeling his way—
getting into the engine properly and wholeheartedly. He'd
handled her before, on the way out from New Alex, but
that was only a guest spot. This was for real. She was his
baby now. He was fusing his personality with her just as
I fused mine with the whole being that was the *Hooded
Swan*.

I caressed the load gently, playing with the awesome power of the driver. The relaxation field never drew tight. The deration-plasm was in equilibrium every inch of the way. Sam was brilliant, as I'd known he would be. He had got himself right into the drive in a matter of moments, and I knew we weren't going to wobble and have to take the approach a second time. We made a perfect transfer, and I began to denature the mass swiftly, easing us into a nice steady six thou. At that rate, it would only be a matter of minutes before I had to take her back down and prepare for the run-up to the nebula.

We were right out of reach now.

Out of sight, though not out of mind. They would all be awake now, back at the base, wondering what the hell was on. But we'd gone. All they had was a blind guess.

"OK, Sam," I said, "rest easy. I'm going to loop us around the nebula. No hurry. Just get the feel of things. There's all the time in the world. I'll slow her to two thou so the flux needs some coaxing. Just look after her. I know it won't take long for you to know this engine as if you'd been sleeping with her all your life, but we'd better just wake up your confidence. You know what the man reckons —getting through the gateway is more of an engineer's *tour de force* than a pilot's. You can call the cards if you want. Just say the word."

"Hang on," he said. "There's a lot of words we seem to have missed out. I got the distinct impression we were running out."

"Running out?" I repeated, slightly puzzled. "You mean running *away*? Good God, no. It never crossed my mind. Of course we're not running away. We're going through that damn lens to look for the *Sister Swan*, and then we're coming back again. We're running out on all the excess baggage, not the job. I want to do this thing my way, not Charlot's. I think my way is better. Why'd you think we were running out altogether?"

"Hell's bells," he said. "You wake me up in the dead of night and tell me we're going to hijack a starship, and we sneak out of the dome, across the surface and into the ship, on tiptoe all the while. We blast off in one hell of a hurry and go supercee in a matter of minutes. What am I supposed to think?"

"Sam," I said, "you have no faith in human nature."

"No," he agreed.

"It's simple enough," I told him. "When you come right down to it, this whole thing is a real sucker play. OK, I'm a sucker. We admit that. You and I know the score, Sam. We know what we're doing, which is more than Titus Charlot, for all his wisdom and his arrogance, can possibly know. Charlot wants to play games, using people for pieces. Not me. If I'm going to be in on a game I want to be the player, not the piece. Charlot bugs me, and I won't let it happen the way he has it down to happen. I can't fly a ship solo and you're elected. Not the kid. He'll have his own chances, in his own time. You get the drift?"

"I get you," he said. "But I only hope you know what you're doing, because if this job louses up there are going to be an awful lot of people spitting at your memory."

"Maybe so," I agreed, "but it's down to me that they're still alive and spitting. Johnny Socoro is never going to forgive me for leaving him out of this, whether I come back or not. But that's not the point."

"OK," said Sam. "It's your funeral. I'm in the coffin for the ride."

"Don't say that," I told him. "Just look on the bright side, if you can find it. Just let's ease the ship through her paces while you feel her up. And, Sam . . ."

"Yeah?"

"Didn't you get a kick out of it? Heisting a starship . . . didn't it feel like the answer to a long-lost cause?"

"As a matter of fact," said the last of the great romantics, "no."

It is a sad truth that many of us are not really at home in the roles which destiny carves out for us.

Even the lowliest of liner-jockeys must feel some sort of pang when he lets his ship be taken out of his own hands. It's like a mother being forced to hand her newborn baby back to a robot nurse for safekeeping. It may be the best thing for all concerned but it's a painful moment. Handing a ship over to a computer is worse, because even a robot nurse has hands. A ship's automatic pilot has only a spool of magnetic tape and a clutch of wires—a series of printed circuits inside a tube is its brain and a pattern of electric pulses meandering around cuprocarbon cytoarchitecture is its action and intelligence. It's not the machine you resent—the machine is an organ of the ship that you love—but the fact that the machine is run by an absent, often anonymous head represented by a set of *rules*. There's no margin for feeling or reaction or sensitivity in a computerized flight-plan.

Nevertheless, as soon as Sam was happy in his harness, I had to bow out and let the automatics take over.

I aligned her along the axis of the lens, dropped her into the prescribed groove, synchronized the timing on the activator, and let her go.

It was probably worse for me than it would have been for anyone else. The *Hooded Swan* was more me than any other ship was anyone else. In addition, I knew what it was like to be a passenger in my own body. I'd had to step aside and let an alien take control of *everything* that was me. I had a comparison to draw. I had the feeling to relate. When Titus Charlot's ghost, personified by a computer program, took over the flight of the *Swan* I felt as though he were cheating the very nature of existence. He seemed far more alien than the wind, at that moment. But it was only a feeling—another waking dream—and it passed.

I sagged in the cradle, exempting myself even from the tension.

My hands were still holding the controls, but the levers eased between my fingers without any pressure from my muscles. I was still participating in that I was still empathizing with the ship, but I felt totally weak and impotent. At any second, as fast as I could react, I could take the volition of the ship back into myself. With a single dramatic action I could override the program and do whatever I had to do. But if we were going to go *through* the gateway instead of just into the nebula and out again I had to trust Charlot's flight-plan. I didn't know how sensitive the gateway might be, but I still remembered one of the most important discoveries of my childhood—the moment that I found circles punched out of sheet alloy in Herault's workshop wouldn't operate slot machines. They just went in and came right out again.

It made little enough difference to Sam. Though I was in suspended animation he was still very much the pacemaker to the ship's heart. He was still wholly involved as we hurtled toward the dead center of the Nightingale. Through the ship's sensors I could see the vast circle of the nebula growing and swelling, billowing out all around our startrack. I could feel the distorted space and the muted timeblast that cocooned us.

It was as though we were vanishing into a gigantic bowl—a tunnel in space with no light visible at the other end. The power of the nebula enfolded us, and the grip of its strained spatial fabric was like bandages or swaddling-clothes.

I felt the anamorphosis that was the substance of the Nightingale's heart fold over my wings as we soared into the center. I felt the wings give, felt them adjust to the soft, fingerless clutch of the contortive domain. The grip was light enough here, like a thin liquid washing over us, or a silk scarf draping our body.

In no time at all, as we went deeper still, the liquid seemed to get more dense, the scarf became a blanket, the clasp became firm and definite. It was no longer a touch but an insistent, smothering pressure. My heartbeat slowed down and I found it difficult to breathe. I had the sensation of drowning, slowly . . . very slowly. . . .

As we'd begun the run we were going no more than point six or seven cee, but we'd climbed steadily, and I could sense the approach of the Einstein barrier. We were well over point nine, approaching ninety-nine and still climbing the asymptote. We could never get to the barrier —we either had to jump it or duck it, but as we came to it time stretched like elastic and the split seconds telescoped, becalming us in instantaneous nowhen.

As a ship accelerates subcee or slows in tachyonic phase the stress in the flux-field increases as the inverse square. The load becomes terrific and the mass-relaxation equation becomes well-nigh impossible to balance. It becomes a matter of juggling with infinitesimals, and no one's even sure that infinitesimals exist. The web becomes highly unstable, and the most delicate of cooperation between pilot, engineer, and drive-unit is imperative. Sam I trusted, and the drive I trusted, but the program . . .

The damp on the relaxation web became so heavy that its manipulability was completely gone.

Suspended, we waited.

I was scared.

The waiting for that vital climactic moment seemed endless. I'd never been so close to the barrier before—if

I'd been transferring phase I would have jumped long before. It was only a matter of tiny splinters of a second, but I spent every one of those splinters sitting right between Sam Parks's eyes, urging him on frantically to keep our integrity one hundred percent. In clean space we could have juggled a little flux and stayed safe, but in the soulless depths of a cosmic lesion only one hundred percent is good enough. Shiver and you're dead.

I don't have any real idea of the subjective eternity which stretched between the first delicate caress of the nebular contortion and the infinite, irresistible implosion that would either turn us into dust or let us through into the alternate continuum—memory simply isn't equipped to deal with experiences of that type. People aren't built in such a way that they can pretend to be light-rays and savor the full sensation of the masquerade. I only know that the swathing force grew tighter and tighter all the time, that I *did* stop breathing and I *was* caught in a wilderness between heartbeats, and that the synesthetic threshold turned the pain into a hideous high-pitched scream and a blazing inferno of light.

It was only for the merest instant—it left hardly any impression on me at all. If I had a real memory of it, even the memory might hurt. But all I have is the faintest echo and a vague impression of having been torn apart and reassembled.

The fabric of space parted and shredded, and we were into the climax, all savage pain and fear. Some kind of orgasmic reflex flowered all around us, the pressure that was collapsing our very molecules everted itself somehow, and the very *form* of existence changed. We became the nucleus of a chain-reaction which ripped reality and cast us adrift in chaos.

It would have to be meaningless to speak of time being spent *crossing over*. Time had no existence any more than there was "space" to be crossed. But there was sensation, in between the dimensions. Something happened . . . my mind was invaded by *something* . . . I participated in an event. We *did* cross over.

While we crossed the interface between existences I think the *Hooded Swan* became a universe in her own right. As a part of her, I too was a universal being. I was everywhere and everything. If, while the *Hooded Swan* is a ship,

I am her soul, then when the *Hooded Swan* was a universe
I was her god. Yet still impotent. Frozen into inaction, not
daring to exercise the least effort of my will, forced to let
existence be reigned by a program that was only a system
of rules built into a machine-subconscious. There was no
question of omnipotence.

Sam, I think, must have felt the whole crossing differently. My involvement with the ship was primarily a sensory involvement—an integration of consciousness and
reaction. His symbiosis was more corporeal in kind. Below
consciousness . . . a different fusion of being. I do not
know what he retained in his own self of that *in between,*
but I know that he must have felt something.

My life stopped when the universe shattered around me.
It began again when the new reality converged.

It was created, or so it seemed, out of nothing: whole
and complete and dynamic. The creation was instantaneous.

I had expected the unexpected. I had been warned that
this was *the* crucial moment. I had deliberately avoided
making guesses, forming ideas. I wanted no preconceptions.
I wanted to be as free as was humanly possible, to react,
and react *right*. *This* was the moment that had proved too
much for Eve.

All I knew was that I was going into another universe.
But as Titus Charlot had suspected, other universes are
not necessarily similar to our own.

Not at all. . . .

XII

"Sam!" I yelled, and I dumped every last fraction of the load we were carrying into the flux-field. I knew he couldn't handle it and I knew the panic-stricken yell wasn't going to help him any, but it was all I could do.

At supercee we'd have been smashed, but we were ninety-nine and climbing down. The flood that Sam couldn't dissipate shook us and shuddered us, but without phase-flicker it didn't manage to break our back.

There's an old joke about a fall never hurting anybody —it's always the abrupt stop at the end. Not very funny. It's not funny at all when you go through a hole expecting to find emptiness and run straight into a brick wall.

It might just as well have been a brick wall—almost. When you're traveling as fast as we were, an impact with a thin ion cloud can be enough to spread you like strawberry jam.

It didn't kill us. That was because I was good, and Sam was good, and we were both lucky. It didn't kill us, but it damn near took my soul to pieces.

I turned into a human torch.

My skin was flaring, crisping like paper ash, turning to lead. There was a terrible shock, and a renewal of all the pressure which I'd only that moment escaped.

Then I was drenched with a horrible cold numbness, and I felt that I'd taken a strong dose of death. But that, too, was only partial. It took me and it left me, and somehow, we stopped.

The space we came into had three dimensions. It contained us. But in the first few minutes that was just about all I could be sure of. Our universe is virtually empty— the amount of matter drifting about in all that vacuum is very small indeed. If the land beyond the lens was empty of matter, then it certainly had some very tough space. I couldn't help the notion that we'd dived through the hole into thick soup. I knew that was nonsense—if we'd really come through into matter-dense space we'd have had no chance—but I couldn't help the analogy. There was no other analogy to be used. The *Hooded Swan* was built to fly, but she couldn't fly here. At best, she could swim, and coming in from the mouth of the Nightingale we were very definitely going against the current.

The flux bled, and the drive-chamber only just held out. It can't have been more than a whisker away from cracking strain. If it *had* cracked, Sam would have been fried, just as Lapthorn had been fried when I smashed the tail of the *Javelin* trying for a hopeless landing. I guessed, even then, what had happened to the *Sister Swan*. Even then, I was in a position to see the terrible irony implicit in such a fate. Eve Lapthorn just wasn't as fast as me. There was no way she could have been. She'd blasted the flux clean out of the engine, and killed Rothgar just as her brother had been killed. All this I understood in the instant of realization.

The lights went out and the gee-field cut off. I lost the best part of my outer-skin sensors. Nothing came in through the contacts in my neck except noise. Through the hood, I couldn't see anything that made any kind of sense.

I fluttered her wings to bring her around in a curve, to discover whether she was still moving, or whether she was even still capable of movement. With what was left of my stripped senses I tried to judge the forces inherent in the alien space. I tried to test currents and distortive waves. Whether it was the injured sensors, or the nature of the outside environment, or just me, I couldn't tell, but I just felt giddy and I couldn't fix anything in my mind. I had to rip the hood from my head and peel the contacts off my neck. Even after I was cut off, it seemed that the contents of my head were garbled. I tried to see out into the darkness, but even the telltale lights on the instrument panel were going round and round.

"Grainger," grated Sam. "You OK?"

"No," I said. I didn't feel that I could say any more.

Time passed by. Real time. Actual duration. The sense of order that simple temporal location brought to me was enough to set me on the road to recovery. I lay back in the cradle and let a sense of well-being slowly permeate my skin. I had my eyes shut and my fists clenched. I began to feel the cold wetness of my face as the sweat began to evaporate. The dizziness faded.

Down below, all the power was finally drained from the web. Even without touching the controls, I knew when the ship went dead. The lifelessness just folded itself around me. I had an image of the ship frozen into an iceberg or trapped in a block of amber. A grotesque fancy paperweight.

"Sam?" I said.

"Still here," he assured me.

"I'm OK now. You?"

"Shaken," he said, "but not stirred. Burned my hands. Little blisters. Be OK with some cream. OK. No fuss."

"We'll settle for that," I said. "I'm OK. Sympathetic reactions is all. I'm used to it. The bruises'll fade. How bad are things down there?"

"Not too bad. Needs work. Some spares. Nothing we can't take care of out of stores."

"We can patch it between us?"

"Take time. We can put it together again. How are things your end?"

"I don't rightly know," I told him. "Sensors out. Lights and gee completely gone. No auxiliary power at all up here except the telltales. Nerve-net's broken. Lots of connections need redrawing, if only I can figure out which ones and how. When we have power back I can find out how bad the situation is and how much of a miracle we'll need to fix it up. What happens then, I don't know. We hope, or we think of something really clever. I don't know."

"What's it look like out there?" he wanted to know.

"It doesn't," I told him. "I couldn't get anything but noise. Chaos. Could be synesthetic, could be the net going out. I couldn't get a glimpse of anything. No light, no shape. I could feel it—that's all. Felt like treacle . . . no, more like molten glass. Heavy, without being sticky, if you see what I mean. What it means . . . I just don't know. I can't tell, without a straight look."

There was silence for a moment.

"You think we made it?" he asked.

It was a good question. "We might be making it," I

said, "but we're hardly out of the starting gate yet. You don't get to be a hero that easy. You always got to go through hell and back."

"Great," he said.

"We're already staring one failure in the face," I said ruminatively.

"What's that?" he asked.

"The failure of imagination," I told him. "Another universe, we said. Just like that—nothing in particular, only another universe. We knew it would be alien. We suspected it might not be like ours. But hell . . . just how far *can* you jump a conclusion? Everybody's imagination has horizons. One kind or another. Even Titus Charlot's. To him, 'alien' only means another problem to be solved. But the word covers a multitude of strange things . . . the Anacaona, for instance . . . never mind that now, though. The thing is, Sam—you've seen aliens while you've been in space. Weird things. Things maybe beyond your comprehension—I've sure as hell seen things beyond mine. But beyond me there's an awful lot of territory, and no matter how far back I push the limits of my understanding there'll be still more territory opening up. That goes for Charlot too. The aliens I know are only just across the street from us, galactically and conceptually speaking. This may be something else, Sam. We may not even be able to think about this. I don't know. Hell, Sam, the so-called laws of nature around these parts may not even permit us to exist. . . . "

"Cool it," he advised.

"I'm cool," I assured him. "Cool enough."

"Shall I come up there?" he asked.

"OK," I said. "Come up and bring some coffee. We'll lick our wounds and count our dead a while before we decide whether the next step's a snake or a ladder. I guess we can spare that much time."

He closed the circuit down his end. I opened it up full, casting around looking for the *Sister Swan*'s beep. I opened up our artificial ears to anything and everything, but we didn't even pick up noise. From that I judged that substantial parts of the set were kaput. I wasn't sure how much it mattered. Maybe we wouldn't have been able to pick up the beep anyway. Who could tell? The next step seemed to be to open up the panels and try to rig the in-ship power so that we had light and didn't float. We weren't right out—the instruments were still registering, even though what they registered didn't signify much. The life-support systems were still operating—air and temperature control, at least. And the control-to-drive circuit. I only hoped Sam would find enough power somewhere to heat up the coffee. In the end, rather than dive right into the heart of the problem, I simply got a big flashlight and settled for being able to see.

I swung the hood right back out of my way and unstrapped myself from the cradle. I had to move slowly, keeping my hands on the column, until I found my no-gee feet. Then I hopped over to one of the couches with no trouble. The inside of the control room looked beautifully stable and sane. All the walls were flat and the angles were square. Everything was nice and solid. We could have been anywhere in the known universe . . . or out of it. The *Hooded Swan*, at least, was a pocket of reality wherever it was we'd come to. A haven. Perhaps, somewhere out in the unknown, there was another pocket—the sister ship.

What would happen, I wondered, if I went into the airlock, opened it, and looked out? Would I see anything at all? Would I go mad? Would it simply kill me? And if I went out?

I might become another pocket of reality, drifting in nowhere. Or I might be absorbed. Assimilated. Turned inside out. Maybe I couldn't step out. Maybe there wasn't a *where* to step into.

How do *you* feel? I murmured, under my breath.

—It's not easy, he said.

Is that all?

—I feel lonely.

I'm here, I pointed out.

—Fair enough, he said. *We* feel lonely.

There was no point in saying that Sam was also there. I knew what he meant.

What do we do? I asked him

—Whatever's needed. We come to terms with this place. We have to be careful not to overreact. We may not be able to understand, but we can coexist. You don't have to be a ballistics expert to kill a man with a gun.

Your choice of analogies, I said, is not encouraging.

—You know what I mean. Senses are built to work on

inadequate information. However inadequate the information we still have sight and sensation. We can learn to make use of them. We can adapt to this reality in some measure, no matter how different it is to our own.

I wish I had your faith, I said.

—Who needs faith? he asked. Remember, Grainger, what I *am*. I'm not a human being . . . not wholly. I'm a neotenic intellect—capable of adapting to almost any ordered mind-structure. I'm functionally designed to cope with this. If I can't do it, it simply can't be done.

That, I said, is what I'm afraid of.

But he was right, as usual. If you ever have to go to hell, choose your companions well. A human being is conditioned to use himself in a particular way. You have to learn to see and to feel, and to make sense of what your senses tell you. You have to be programmed. And once programmed, you're stuck. It's a tough job unlearning, remaking sense. We all know the classic about the guy with the inverting glasses. He had to learn to see the world the right way up all over again. And yet again, when they took the glasses away. I've heard that if you bring a kitten up from birth in an environment where everything is vertically striped, when you finally show the adult cat a horizontally striped screen it actually *sees* the screen as spotted.

But the wind wasn't that set in his ways. Set enough, perhaps, because he'd been adapting himself to my mind for a long time. But he had vast reservoirs of objectivity that were not available to me. My mind is an ephiphenomenon of my body. His body was an epiphenomenon of my mind. He might not be able to detach himself at will, but he had a degree of detachment nevertheless. If it was possible—and not just humanly possible—to make some kind of sense out of the rules of existence in the alternate continuum, then he could do it. He could reach out and feel his way around. He could use my senses even if I couldn't.

It wasn't the first time I'd been glad to have him around. There was no one I'd rather have inside me in a mess like this one.

If we take a look, I said, can you give me a report? Tell me what the chances are?

—In time, he said. Take it easy now. I promise you, I can handle it. It's my line of country. Leave it to me.

He always was an arrogant bastard. And he sure as hell didn't learn it from me. At least, I don't think so.

Sam opened the door. He looked as if his face had been whitewashed. He was carrying coffee in squeezy-bags. Not two, but three.

"Look what I've found," he said. I've never seen a sicker smile.

She walked into the control room, as cool as you like, floating delicately while her legs pedaled slowly, and said, "Where are we?"

XIII

"What in the name of hell are *you* doing here?" I demanded.

"I work here," she said.

"You were on board. Asleep. When we lifted?" I had to pause between phrases. I should have known. It was my business to know. A captain ought to know exactly where his crew is. Especially if they're on his ship.

It seemed that we could add kidnapping to the list of our heinous crimes.

My grip tightened about the strap I was holding on to while I sat and looked at her. I wondered what my face must look like. She eased herself around the couch behind mine and sat down. She moved with almost preternatural ease in the geeless conditions. She probably didn't weigh a lot under par. She was always light on her feet.

"Miss Vogan," I said, "do you have any idea what's happened since you tucked yourself in a few hours back?"

"I know," she said.

"I don't think you do," I told her. Sam gave me my coffee, and I held it firmly, feeling the warmth against the flesh of my palm. I didn't try to drink any of it.

"I don't think you do," I repeated, "because if you do why aren't you frightened half to death?"

"I am," she assured me. For a brief second, she looked it. Her eyes could no longer meet mine, and when she dropped them, just for an instant, there was the bright light of fear shining in them. But she had self-control. Probably more than I had. I must have had strain written all over me.

I suddenly felt a wave of horror. "I'm sorry," I said, pushing the words out hard. "God, I'm sorry."

"Why?" she said.

"I didn't know you were on board."

"It makes no difference," she told me. "I was scheduled to make the trip, remember? I signed on for this."

"It makes a difference to me," I said harshly.

"It shouldn't," she answered, with an edge to her own voice.

"There was no point," I murmured, in a hardly audible voice. I coughed and spoke a little louder. "There was no need to risk any more lives. Two is plenty. Two is enough."

She actually glared at me. She couldn't sustain the glare, but the thought was there, and in situations like that, it's the thought that counts.

"You didn't bother to *ask* whether I wanted my life saved."

"No," I admitted. "No, I didn't. I'm sorry. Which is what I said in the first place. Let's forget it. We're here, and you're here. Let's just drink our coffee and try to take it as it lies."

I stuck the end of the tube into my mouth and released the valve at the neck. The coffee tasted good. It compensated for a lot of uneasiness.

"We could need her," said Sam, after a while. "There's a hell of a lot of work needs doing before this tub is fit to limp home, and anywhere else we might have to go in the meantime. Three pairs of hands . . . "

" . . . is one pair more than two pairs," I finished. "Sure."

She didn't say a word, but in her thoughts she wasn't thanking me. I couldn't tell whether she was working off some of her tension in anger and hostility or whether she really did resent my attempt to leave her at home. Probably both. These days, it seems, everybody wants to be a hero. With the starways opening up and unlimited opportunity on every hand, everybody has galaxy-sized ambitions. Nobody sees any limits. Nobody has a sense of proportion anymore. The expanding horizons of the imagination. Out, out, and away. Deep space is everybody's plaything. You too can have your own private nova.

I could hardly blame her. Who was I to predict that disillusionment was just around the corner?

I don't think I was ever young. I wonder if I missed something.

Afterward, I was reluctant to move. We'd followed the coffee with a fistful of gruel, but somehow it hadn't fixed me up ready to face infinity with a light heart. Hesitation, of course, is all very well when you have a range of action from which to choose. But this was a time for creating choices, not for sitting back and waiting for them to arrive. I had to overcome my reluctance and get moving.

I wiped my fingers on my shirt, though they weren't sticky. Then I made for the door.

"What are you going to do?" asked Sam. "Wait until I get the power back."

"I'm going to suit up and take a look out of the airlock," I said. "Nothing drastic. A quick look and then I'll come back. Just stick around. I'll give you the bad news in a matter of minutes."

Nobody criticized me for assuming that the news would be bad. The good news would only start once we got back out of the nebula.

Sam came with me to the lock and he helped me into a suit. I chose the lightest of the suits but I took a heavy opaque helmet with a narrow viewfield-window and a visor with a strong filter. It wasn't much in the way of a precaution but it made me feel better to be planning in advance. Taking decisions improved my self-confidence.

I got into the lock and evacuated it, feeding the air back into the *Swan*. If we were going to be here for some time we couldn't afford to lose oxygen.

Then I eased the outer door open. I was tempted to open it just a crack and peep out one-eyed, but that had a hint of absurdity about it. Instead, I gave it a determined push, and exposed myself deliberately to the universe without.

It *was* bright.

Bright enough, at any rate, for me to leave the filter on, though not bright enough to have hurt me if I hadn't bothered with it. There was a dazzling fringe around the rim of the lock, but *out there* it was only as bright as sunlight. It looked like a hazy sky, colored, with the suggestion of cloud, but when I tried to focus on the cloudiness, the colors all ran and changed. It was like watching the spectra in an oil slick on moving water, only the color distribution wasn't red to indigo. There was more yellow, more white. The starker colors came in flashes and streaks, as though superimposed on a lighter, brighter backdrop. I didn't have to move my head to make the colors stir—it was enough just to change the focus of my attention. It

was as though my very thoughts were being reflected out
there in the non-images which formed and disappeared. I
remembered the starlight coming through the Nightingale
being turned into sound for aesthetic appreciation. I was
used to synesthetic effects, but what was going on out there
was more real than the overlap which sometimes came
through my contacts.

The halo around the edge of the lock was seeping in. The
space in which I stood was being invaded by a cold white
glow. There was a fog forming on my viewshield—a silver,
hazy body of light which cut me off even further from the
colors stirring in the infinite outside. The glow was oozing
all around me, and I could almost feel it flowing over me.

I could see the walls of the lock—solid, viable shapes. I
could see the edge of the hatch and the hinges, but all the
shapes seemed to be absorbing the glow, taking it onto, if
not actually *into* themselves. It was as if their surface were
being licked by a growing fire—an atomic fire, blaze without flame.

I held up my gauntleted hand in front of my face, and I
saw that it was flaring like everything else. I felt no heat
through the thin suit. The gleam grew more definite, but
it was never fierce, and the glow on my visor and my viewshield never blotted out the colors beyond. Every time I
changed the focus of my thoughts, red, blue, and black
would bleed from the gold-and-silver sky, running in rivers
and vortices, swirling, imploding, and vanishing only to re-
appear. There was no periodicity. It was all random. I
could define no areas in space by their behavior.

I lowered my arm to my side again.

I was standing in a cave of fire.

—It's a surface reaction, said the wind. He sounded
calm, authoritative.

We're going to burn up? I said

—No. Did you ever know a firefly to burn in its own
tail-light? The glow is innocuous. It's not atomic conver-
sion. It's a reaction in the space, not in the matter. We're
safe.

Can you make any sense out of it? I asked.

—Give me *time*—I didn't get into your mind in a matter
of moments, remember. It took days, months to reach real
integration. This isn't easy.

Sorry, I said.

—I'm trying, he assured me. I'm reaching out to get the feel of it.

I looked out into the melting sky, trying to find something out there that might mean something.

Gripping the edges of the lock firmly, I eased my body forward, trying to get away from the cocoon of white light without actually casting myself into space. Looking back and forward along the length of the ship, and out along her wing, I could see that every inch of her was shining with the same cold whiteness. We were lit up like a neon bulb.

Very handy for spotting invaders, I thought. If there's anyone out there looking for us.

—I don't think this is gas, said the wind. It doesn't seem as though we're in atmosphere. So it's not simply that the matter in this universe is distributed. There's more to it than that. It's like an ether.

Heavy distortion can often give the impression that space itself has density. One often speaks of *waves* of distortion, or even tides and pools. From the point of view of our pattern of spatial organization this whole continuum could be badly warped. I remembered the sensation of *current* I'd received when we came through. In distorted space the distance between A and B can differ considerably depending on whether you're going from A to B or vice versa. The current might well be the *grain* of space.

—Keep thinking, said the wind.

I don't know, I said. I just can't make it out.

—Time, he said, time.

And for all I knew, that might be haywire too. Almost certainly was. A distortion in space *is* a distortion in time.

I relaxed, allowing the wind to exert what control he could over my optic nerves and the reception centers in my brain. I felt him stirring in my brain.

I felt my eyes straining, as if they were trying to focus on something which just could not be brought into focus.

You're hurting, I told him.

—I know, he said.

My pain was his pain. But he knew what it was *for* and I didn't. I had to grit my teeth, not so much against the pain in my eyes as the nausea in my stomach. Always there was this old reaction against the feel of another mind using some small part of my body.

The haze which hid the universe in light, or tried to, was still getting worse. But it was in the haze and because of the haze that I saw it. I would never have picked it out in the riot of color.

It was a spot of light. An unsteady but stationary point of white light. A star. Like a star. So very like a star, in fact, that I almost felt a kinship with it. Where were the others? I wondered. How could there be a universe with only one star? No stars I could accept, but a single solitary star seemed absurd. How can you have an infinite chaos, bewildering and unknowable, harboring a single star?

It's not a star, I said.

—No, he agreed.

It's the *Sister Swan*.

—It might be.

It *must* be. We're lit up like a star. She must be too. She's the only pocket of common sense in this place except us. It's her. Glowing, suspended out there like us. Flies in amber.

I felt better, having decided that. It was progress. It was a step on the way. A ladder, not a snake. We were still making it, still on the ball. We were winning.

Knowing that one point of light was a starship, not a star, and seeing it clearly now, fixing it in my mind as a point of reference, not losing it in the chaos, not letting my thoughts drift, I began to make up a picture of what I saw. I tried to make it fall into place. I concentrated hard on the ship, and tried to freeze the chaos in and with my mind.

I *reached out* from my self, as the wind had tried to do, not using my eyes, but all my mental power, cutting through the glare which filled my viewshield, reaching . . . beyond. . . .

. . . And I felt a reaction. I felt the colors coming *into* my mind, slipping into me like eels, like threads of thought. I felt the tumultuous confusion reaching into me as I welcomed it, met it. There was an instant of sharing . . .

. . . And a horror-stricken recoil.

It was the wind. He screamed, and pulled me back. The chaos that was crawling into my mind bubbled and seethed, but was cast back.

We were alone again. My eyes were shut tight. There was a hollowness behind them.

What happened? I asked.

—It's a mind, he hissed. It's not a universe—it's a *mind*. We're prisoners in something's mind.

You don't make sense, I told him.

—*It* doesn't make sense. Not me. But it does. It does make sense. That's the worst of it. I can catch it. A glimpse. The semblance of sense. It's *not* beyond understanding. I wish it were. I hope we don't understand it. I pray that we *can't* understand. But . . .

But what?

—Suppose it can understand us!

He was obviously horrified by the thought. It shocked and scared him. I didn't get it.

You're telling me, I said, that this universe *thinks*. It's alive and sentient. It has a mind.

—No! It *is* a mind.

What's the difference?

—All the difference that matters. The difference between you and me. More than that—infinitely more powerful than that. In the final analysis, I'm made out of matter just like you. I'm organization coded into molecular structures, just like you. This isn't even matter, not as we understand it. It's etheric, made of stretched and folded space. It's coded into the very substance of existence. It's *not* a universe—not in any sense that we can understand . . . it's no more a universe than the Nightingale is a nebula. We're in danger here, Grainger . . . deadly danger. If we reach an understanding with the mind we will be destroyed. Utterly. Matter itself is alien to this universe. This mind has all the power of natural law implicit in itself. If you like, it's as powerful as gravity. We're nothing, do you understand? If it can reach us, if it can *understand* us, we'll just cease to exist materially. We're in trouble, Grainger . . . you just can't imagine how much trouble.

That, I thought, is the whole truth and nothing but.

—Shut the hatch! he commanded. Now!

I opened my eyes tentatively, and was almost surprised to find that I could look out into the misty colors without coming to any harm. I could still see the lonely star that might be the *Sister Swan*. I took quite a long, steady look to be sure that it could be done—that I had the self-control *not* to reach out attempting to embrace understanding. I

felt nothing, and I was confident of my ability to keep myself if and when the need arose to look again.

I pulled the hatch closed and locked it. The cave of light
closed around me, and though the glow was dimmed it
did not go out. The volume of the hatch had become a
pocket of the other world within the *Swan*. The alien universe still enclosed me. I felt as though I were suspended
in a jewel-like drop of water, whose every facet shone with
sunlight reflected and refracted. I felt like a microbe or a
speck of dust.

I activated the pumps to clear the lock—expelling whatever was within to the great outside. The glow faded, but
I couldn't know whether it was the effect of the pump—
which surely had nothing to pump—or whether the alien
vacuum was being slowly unwarped into conformity by the
enveloping solidity of sane matter.

Either way, I was prepared to wait until the glow was
quite gone and I was in utter darkness before I took the
risk of opening the inner door.

It did not seem to take very long.

Eventually, I let the air stream back into the lock. A
few seconds passed while the chamber filled and the pressure was equalized. In that time, the wind said nothing at
all. Something had shocked him, hard and deep. The alien
universe might harbor no monsters, no visible perils, no
lethal radiations . . . but it was nevertheless totally inimical
to human life. And his life. Particularly, perhaps, to his
life.

You know we have to go out there again, I said. I don't
know how long for, but long enough. We have no choice.

—I know, he said. We have to take our chance. I can't
tell what chance we have. We just take a blind leap and we
hope.

He was calm and sober. He was also afraid. For once—
and maybe for the one and only time—he was in this as
deep as I was. Maybe deeper. The threat that was posed
was certainly no less a threat to him than to me, and perhaps much more so—he, after all, was designed to be
adaptable, to conform to the prevailing regime. He hadn't
my rigidity, and he hadn't the solid, bodily base and total
integration with that base that I had. The difference between us now left him more exposed than me.

—We have to avoid the patterns, he said.

Patterns?

—That's what thought *is*, he amplified. That's what *life* is. Patterns of molecules, patterns of cells. Order, in an entropic environment. A countercurrent to the flow of randomness. Every thought that passes through your brain —mine as well as yours—is simply an electrical pattern set up in the cytoarchitecture of the gray matter. The coding capacity of that cellular network is vast—well-nigh infinite. There's an incalculable number of thoughts which you might think but never will. But the potential of the network is by no means all-conclusive. There are thoughts which *cannot* be coded into your brain. There are concepts you can't reach. No matter, in most situations . . . a purely hypothetical case. But not here. Here, the patterns which exist in nature—*all of them*—are alien to the very structure of your being. If your mind tries to adapt itself to them it will be destroyed. The whole integration of your thought-processes will be broken down. You need some confirmation, you see, in your environment, to keep the structure of your mind whole and sane. Even in the real world—our world—people lose control . . . their pattern-structure breaks down or is injured. Insanity is never far away even in the world which made us. Here . . . it's going to take every last vestige of faith and strength and luck to hold us together. Physically, as well as mentally. This assault is mounted on all fronts. The only help we have is the ship —maybe both ships. They're our sort of existence, our sort of pattern. They confirm our existence . . . just so long as they maintain their own. But out there, trying to cross from one ship to the other . . . I don't know.

You said something about a mind, I reminded him. You said that this place is a mind.

—I think so. I may be wrong, but I think I'm right. It's trying to assimilate us. Consciously *trying*. Physically, I don't suppose that matters much—it will be as much at the mercy of its own subconscious processes as you are . . . or were, before I joined you. But mentally, it puts us in worse trouble. It means that we're not just exercising our strength against inert force. We're going to be invaded . . . we're going to be mindpicked.

He already knew what I thought about mindpicking— he knew that the use of the word would frighten me more than his cold logic and his wordy theory. He was trying to make me see just how badly off we were . . . or might be.

You don't want to try, do you? I said.

—I'm only . . .

Only nothing. You want to turn back now. You don't want to try to reach the *Sister Swan*. You want to run.

—It might be an idea, he said.

You're supposed to be the hero, I reminded him. I'm the guy you're always kicking for lack of violent enterprise and reckless courage, remember.

—I remember, he said.

This is different, I added for him. This time your neck's out with mine. Maybe farther than mine. How does it feel to be in my shoes? How do you feel, hero?

—If the positions are reversed, said the wind, then we should both be in a position to understand. How do *you* feel?

Not so heroic.

—But you're going to make the attempt.

That's right.

—So OK. But you aren't going to say I didn't warn you. You're going to remember—if you get the chance to remember—that the time I acted your part, you acted mine. I want you to remember that. Just so you'll know. We really are in this together. Not just *this*, but all of it. Life, existence. You and I, brother. We're no different, under the skin.

I'll remember what there is to remember, I told him.

—Remember this, he said. There's something out there. Maybe alive, maybe dead. Maybe thinking, perhaps not. But there's something which reached into your brain and tried to communicate, when you let it. If you let it do it again . . . well, perhaps you won't. But even so, you can't ignore the possibility that it *knows*. It has you tagged. No matter where you try to hide, it has you covered. Think about that.

I'm thinking.

—I can't help you. Not this time. If anything, it's you who have to help me. You have to lend me your strength.

And if I refuse, I said—on impulse—I might just get rid of you. This just could be my chance.

—If you want to look at it that way, he said. I don't think you do.

You're betting your life on that chance, I pointed out.

—It's not that simple, he assured me. You weigh it up. We're on the same side, Grainger. You know that now. You've known for some time. We're friends now.

He was right, and I knew it. Come the moment he needed my help, he'd have it. If it wasn't enough . . . well, we'd probably both be dead. There was no getting around it—he'd infected me. One hundred percent. I'd always feared ending up something that wasn't really me, and here I was. We were finally playing interchangeable parts. Grainger I and Grainger II. What a double act.

You're never alone . . . with a parasite.

XIV

———◆———

"Miss Vogan," I said, much later, "can you fly a star-ship?"

"From the pilot's seat?" she asked.

"Where else?"

"No."

"You mean no?" I persisted. "You really have no idea? You honestly couldn't give me a definite maybe?"

The tone of my voice was flippant, but hard. She looked at me as if I might be crazy. She wasn't used to my death-watch manner. She'd seen too many HV dramas dripping with nobility and hysteria.

"I can't pilot a ship," she said dogmatically.

"What's this all about?" said Sam. He was half out of sight inside the casing of the drive integration systems. We had light by this time and enough gee to keep our feet on the floor. Piece by piece, the *Swan* was coming back to life. Our chances were getting better. The one thing we couldn't touch was the nerve-net, which didn't really fall into Sam's province or mine. But I had my own ideas about who might be able to fix that for us. There were, however, precautions to be taken.

"You know damn well, Sam," I said. "I'm going to take a little ride and I just might not come back. If that happens, you're going to have to go home on your own to tell the tale. Miss Vogan is unfortunately with us, she might per-form the one task which could conceivably be useful. She can sit in the cradle and sync in the computer rerun which just might—if Heaven is on our side—get you out of this oil-slick soup and back to lovable vacuum . . . from which, no doubt, heroes will be lining up to rescue you."

"The *Sister Swan* could have a crew," said Sam. "We have a ship. Wouldn't we have a better chance trying a second time to reach her? If, as you seem bent on assuming, you don't."

"No," I said.

"If you're dead," said Mina, "it can hardly be your decision."

"Sweet little thing, aren't you?" I said. "I'm the captain and you'll bloody well do as you're told, whether I die after I tell you or not. Right?"

She didn't say a word. Sam, with his head out of the way, could legitimately ignore me.

"All right," I said, "we'll do it by logic. If I don't make it something out there will have stopped me. If it stopped me it will stop you. That's one count. If it's not enough you can add this one: if it kills me, it probably killed *them* weeks ago. They've been here a lot longer than we have, remember. If I don't come back, you go home. You *try* to go home. It may be as long a chance as any other, but it's the only trick worth trying. OK?"

Sam emerged. His face was white under the grease smears. He looked even more like a long, thin white shadow than ever. A ghost already, while he was still alive.

"Would it double up your chances if I came with you to the sister ship?" he asked.

"No," I said, quite definitely.

"Then I guess the only thing to do is go home," he said. "But we'll give you a good long wait. We don't want to leave you behind, now do we?"

"No," I said again, just as definitely, but in a different kind of voice.

"Fine," I said. "You come with me." The last remark, of course, was addressed to the girl.

I took her up to the control room, sat her in the cradle, and I explained very carefully how the computer was engaged and under what conditions it ought to be engaged. In a matter of minutes, without demonstration or simulation, I tried to explain to her how to handle a ship. She must have heard it all before—in theory—and I was uncomfortably aware that what I was telling her now would be just as useless as it was then. I knew she couldn't do it just as well as she did.

But when all else fails there's nothing to hope for except the miracles, and even miracles need a helping hand. I

hoped fervently that all else wasn't *going* to fail, but I
was quite determined that I wasn't going to play the blind
man. This was my show and it was going to be run my way
whether I was around to run it or not. Sure it wasn't fair,
on Sam or the girl, but when is it *ever* fair?

She was wishing she was at home long before I was
finished with her. She hadn't expected it to be like it was.
If Titus Charlot had been aboard, it probably wouldn't
have been. She was in the wrong screenplay, really—she'd
have been more at home in Charlot's version.

After the lesson in elementary piloting, we had more
work to do on the ship. I wanted her well on the way to
health before I sallied forth to pick up the passengers.
There was no point in bringing them back to a wreck. I had
a shrewd suspicion that they wouldn't be in any fit condition to buckle down and help us sort things out, although
I knew full well that some of our hopes were going to have
to lie in that direction. Without Nick delArco, we were
nine-tenths dead. The *Hooded Swan* was a superb ship,
whose performance was way ahead of anything else known
to humankind—or to the Khor-monsa. She could do things
no other ship could dream about. But there's a price to be
paid for that kind of performance. The bird wasn't delicate
but she was sure as hell intricate. The integration of all
her systems was so terribly complicated that Sam and I,
even added together, couldn't make a complete job of jury-
rigging her. We needed someone with special knowledge—
a ship designer, like Charlot, or a ship-builder . . . like Nick
delArco.

If he was dead, or mad, or I couldn't get him back here,
then it might just as well be Mina Vogan at the controls as
me. Whoever it was would be flying blind and senseless,
with no guide but Fate. With a record like mine, I could
hardly be expected to put much faith in Fate.

All in all, the situation was as rough as hell. I had to
play the hero, no matter what the wind thought, because
I was in too deep not to. I needed Nick delArco. The
absurdity of that was quite ironic. The idea of needing
Nick delArco had never occurred to me before.

I worked away for I don't know how long. Sam worked
too, mostly separately. Mina Vogan fluttered back and
forth like a moth, lending a hand here and a hand there.
No words of encouragement, though. She was no Florence

Nightingale. I think I was thankful for that. Her dourness
fitted in well. Over a period of time, I watched the stress
ease out of her face, to be replaced by a haunted expression
which signified compromise with the inevitable. Though I
hardly exchanged half a dozen words with her I knew what
was going on in her mind. She was in full retreat, with-
drawing into the necessity of the situation. Step by step she
came down from the elevated position where she could
command a view of the possibilities which lay before us.
She stopped thinking about what might happen tomorrow,
or in the next ten minutes. She let something that was
mechanical take over the running of her body. She resigned
all responsibility for the horrible mess we were in. Eventually, she was quite calm. Cruising in low gear. I watched
the change come over her with a macabre intellectual
interest. I wondered what that sort of change signified in
terms of what was *out there*. Was she rendering herself
vulnerable to it, or immune from it? I couldn't tell. Time
might, but I hoped that it wouldn't come to that.

No similar change came over Sam. He had less natural
self-assertion and less need to lose it, but quite apart from
that he retained the courage and the determination to live
this thing through. When we faced each other again, for a
brief and silent meal, I watched him closely, and I could
see that he was still participating. He was still thinking . . .
he could still see all the angles.

I felt proud of Sam. I don't know why . . . there was
no reason why *I* should find anything to be proud of. But
I was pleased. I felt sorry for Mina. The fact that she'd
tried to rub me up the wrong way was neither here nor
there.

Personally, I was scared rigid. I couldn't climb down
from my lofty pinnacle of vantage over the possibilities,
because it was largely my actions that were going to steer
us through them. I was stuck. In a sense, my reaction was
more like Mina's than Sam's. I was compromised by the
inevitable. If anybody aboard the *Hooded Swan* was a
real hero, it had to be Sam. But he, of course, was the
guy who'd always nurtured a yen to be one alongside a
keen appreciation of the reasons why he wasn't. Sam made
sense. I'm not sure that I did. I only ever wanted a quiet,
lonely life.

XV

I wore a light suit, unshielded, and a helmet, opaque except for the eyepiece, with a dark filter. The measure of protection with which I attempted to guard myself from the mind-invading force was primarily internal. There were two possible strategies by which I could attempt to armor my mind. I could attempt to strengthen it in order to withstand the onslaught, or I could attempt to conceal it, in order to confuse the attacker. The first strategy required augMENTation, the second disruption. I chose the latter. I had two excuses for this choice: the first, that I had a strong prejudice against augMENTation; the second, that I feared my own capacity for understanding more than the hypothetical capacity of the alien continuum. With the second of these reasons the wind was in whole-hearted accord. He, too, preferred to befuddle his mind rather than place himself at the mercy of its reflexes.

The only trouble was that I dared not shoot myself brim-full of a hallucinogen or a psychedelic. I wanted to be high, but not so high that I couldn't do what I had to. I needed a measure of sanity.

I chose, in the end, a metabolic anti-catalyst that would slow me down and make it difficult to think, but which would allow me to think logically. The same drug would reduce my oxygen-need, and could make a vital contribution to the potential success of the mission in that way too. I didn't know how long I was going to be out there.

In order to carry me through the ether to the other ship, I used a standard torpedo—a miniature spaceship with controls outside. It wasn't capable of great velocity, but I just had to take a chance on its being adequate for my needs. I also took a hand power-gun for propelling myself about the *Sister Swan* if and when I got there.

I sat on the torpedo in the airlock for a couple of minutes, watching the glow seep in and flare up, waiting for the machine to grow a halo. Then I nudged myself out and looked back to see the whole beautiful body of the Swan bathing in a cloud of white light, more like an angel than a bird. I was just the tiniest of baby stars, a spark hurled out into a multicolored night by a fierce blaze to drift in the smoke and dance on the circulating air.

I picked out the star that might be the *Sister Swan*. It looked very far away indeed, though only my imagination fueled my judgment. There was no standard for comparison. I pointed myself toward it, fixing my attention upon it while the fog was building up on my visor. I tried not to look at the colored chaos—tried to be unconscious of the reflection of my thoughts in the sky—but I couldn't help knowing they were there, and knowing the threat that they posed. I forced as much of my attention as was possible on the single speck of stardust, and tried to hypnotize myself by it.

Though the effect of the drug upon my body was fairly stable, the effect on my time-sense was not. Ordinarily, this would be a most unwelcome side effect in the use of the drug, but at the moment it could prove valuable. I felt very sluggish, as though my mind were floating on treacle. I felt as if I might be the size of a mountain one moment, and an ant the next. My consciousness swayed, pendulum fashion. I could not make out whether I weighed a million tons, or whether I was nothing and a million tons was pressing in upon me from all sides, squeezing me into collapsed matter.

After the one glance, I didn't look back, but that one glance might have taken minutes or hours. In the alien continuum I was adrift from environmental time, and because of the drug I was partially separated from metabolic time.

The colored world closed around me. It really was a tunnel, now, with a speck of light at one end, and a speck of light at the other. I was in motion between the two points, but *where* I might be relative to either of them was unknowable, and perhaps unanswerable. It didn't matter. All that mattered in this entire universe were the two points of light and the chrysalises of reality which they enfolded. The point of light toward which I was traveling did not grow. There was nothing to tell me that I was getting closer.

I began to sense something of the curvature of space around me.

I felt a slow giddiness bubbling in the depths of my mind. It seemed to be just beneath the hind-brain, in the pons or the pineal body. It was like a gyroscope, spinning. A still-center around which the universe Catherine-wheeled. The sensation of turning proved *irresistible,* and the flood of the clouds began to describe a circular path around the sky. The circle itself began to spin, and became a globe. The globe began to spin . . . and my mind revolted. The circle and the globe began to stretch and distort, became unduloid and catenoid, and folded back Klein-bottle fashion into a nodoid surface . . . still my mind revolted and re-coiled. I could not stretch myself to accommodate or con-form to the shape of this alien space. The clouded colors could not betray my eyes, which remained focused on the star.

A far-distant nausea washed the shores of my being. I could not fall down my spinal column to enjoin with the sickness. My gut was miles away, buried deep in substance with the texture of inert rock. Not the merest tremor could rise to startle my concentration. I was aware of the unease, but the drug held me all but invulnerable.

—It's coming, said the wind.

His soulless voice was slow and ponderous. It seemed to *roll* around the inside of my skull, sonorous and echoless.

—It's like a wind, he said. A wind getting in my being. Coming through me and over me. Pulling me.

I felt it. I felt my command over eternity beginning to melt. His words were damp, they sagged, they spread, and they lost their coherence. The world was crumbling.

Fight it, I said.

I was demanding resistance from myself as much as from the wind. I felt my words fracturing into sibilant phonemes, each one dissolving like sugar in sulfuric acid. I felt myself invaded.

I was adrift in a kaleidoscope, and the ever-shifting pat-terns were trying to engulf and incorporate me. I had thought that the colors reflected the incidence of my own mind upon the aspect of the sky . . . now I saw that it might well be the other way around, that the changing

quality of the sky was stirring my thoughts and my being,
stretching, attempting to tear and split, agitating and dis-
turbing.

The iridescence which surrounded me tried to strike
into me. I foresaw the surface of my mind rupturing, fur-
rowing, cracking like drying mud. I felt myself dragged
toward that possible future, hauled into accepting it. I resisted.

I felt the polychromatic wilderness oozing into the
fissures of my consciousness, sucking at the layers of my
organized being, extending silvery threads into unsuspected
crevices, tightening its hold, extending its grip, increasing its
leverage. I felt tentacles thrusting and searching like wet
white worms, pulpy and soft and cold and elastic, plumb-
ing the depths of my waking dream.

I sensed abyssal depths beneath me, beside me . . .
chasmic claws reaching for my heart from all directions.
The gulfs filled with light and colors and it was flooding
me . . . dissolving me. . . .

From the impermanent future I tried to escape into the
rigid past, to reverse the invasion and hurl myself away
from it. But I was trapped between the giant grinding mill-
wheel of alternativity.

The decorated limbo through which I dived interlaced
the fragments of my mind. It was pulling me apart.

But very slowly. I felt my blessed heaviness, my ultimate
immovability. The moment in which I was trapped ex-
ploded and stretched. The chaos strained in vain. I was
invited into the ravelment of the alien universe, but I
refused. I could not be drawn. I was winning the battle.

I resisted with all the kinds of strength I had. Self-
knowledge, self-assurance, self-love. I gathered myself into
what I knew and I held it. I could not exempt myself from
the ectopic force but I could match it. I could counter-
balance it. Its energies poured into the sensory scissures of
my being, but I gripped and contained them. They could
not and would not burst my soul.

There was a tremulous hum spilling through my senses,
and I knew that the wind was trying to shape words which
refused to take form. I had to trap the sounds and squeeze
the meaning out of them.

—Help me, he was saying, help me . . .

The fight that I was winning, he was losing.

He didn't have my strength of self-preservation. He didn't have my level of self-awareness. He was a creature of many selves. He was fighting with all he could borrow from me, but it could not be enough. Nothing short of total fusion could give him the resources I had. And that was beyond his capabilities. He was a facultative parasite. My death was not his . . . he could go on to another host. The price which he paid for that immortality was the difference between the level of integration which he had and the level which he needed.

—Help me, he said. Crying in anguish.

I tried. I tried to include him in my own wall of defense. But it couldn't be done. There was no way. I couldn't take him into myself. I couldn't include him in my concept of self. To me, he was an alien. He always had been, I could think of him no other way. With all the will in the world, I could not help him.

I can't, I said.

My voice was like thunder.

He screamed.

—Please!

The word boomed, stretched, sank.

I can't.

For the first time, I felt him inside my skull. Like a rat scurrying in the gullies of my subconscious. Something lurking inside me. Something . . . I could not help the thought . . . evil. I felt the pressure of him extenuating in my mind, a force that slid and shifted like a snake.

Don't!

He screamed again.

—*Help me!*

It was a whine, stridulant, lacerating the inner ears with which I listened.

But there was no way. I just couldn't

Unbidden, words bubbled out of me. Silent words, cascading, splashing, shattering. A waterfall of thoughts, imperfectly vocalized, incoherent. Verbal foam. I was trying to explain. I was trying to make excuses. The words just spewed out, mangled and dying. I couldn't tell him. I couldn't even tell him I was sorry.

But he was still screaming. He was still agonized, still blazing with fear. But his words were whole. His being was whole. It came to me that he was stronger than he thought.

He was surviving. It wasn't breaking him. The force of his need to live, the force of his appeal for help.

He wasn't dying.

I screamed at him, hurled words into the tumultuous gulf trying to make him understand.

We were too far apart. We couldn't communicate. The iridian infinity boiling in my brain swept us apart and would not let us touch.

And . . .

. . . I was falling into a star . . . falling into the gaping maw of a cosmic fire. For a moment, I thought I was burning. Then I realized that the star had the form of a gigantic bird, wings spread, neck stretched. Flaming like a phoenix . . .

. . . Although it was a swan.

XVI

I was again engulfed by the white radiance. The torpedo, guided almost subconsciously, carried me *into* the belly of the *Sister Swan*. I backblasted the motor for an instant to cancel my momentum, but I was too slow to stop the nose of the missile striking a metal face. The jar jerked me forward from the saddle of the machine, and for a moment the *real* vertigo eclipsed the alien invader in my mind. The colored chaos was flushed out, leached from my soul.

I began to see again, though the resplendent shine made it difficult to define shape. When I got it all straight in my head, though, I felt a sudden crushing sensation of tragedy.

I had, indeed, been carried *inside* the ship. The entire hind end had been blown open by an explosion, and I was in the wrecked cavern of the loading bay. When Eve dumped the flux as she came through the lens one of the cannons had been flooded and blown out. Bits of the engine room had been thrown out and embedded in the walls of the bay, and what was left was just debris, blooming out from a hole in the tail-section that looked like a bell-flower.

I let the torpedo float free, and it bumped the wall of the bay twice more, but only gently.

I peered through the gap in the bulkhead, into the smashed-up engine room. Ironically . . . horrifically . . . the shape of Rothgar's body was stark and clear, hewn out of silver light. The flux had flooded him and frozen around him in a thick shell, burning his flesh to a crisp but preserving his erstwhile image for all eternity.

Eternity? Suddenly, I wasn't so sure.

My mind retreated a little to the moment when the torpedo had hit the metal face . . . and the two little bumps thereafter. *The wall had given before the impact.*

I was slow. There was a drug swilling around my system *making* me slow. It was difficult to see the problem, to face it, to begin to evaluate it. I was mountain-sized and just as cumbersome while a wave of despair cut slowly through my soul.

Eventually, I was able to reach out and touch the image of Rothgar preserved by the flux and bathed by the silver light.

It crumbled. It was soft, corroded.

The force which had invaded my mind had invaded the being of the *Sister Swan*. I remembered what the wind had said. The pressure was physical as well as mental. Matter itself was alien to this continuum.

The *Sister Swan* was being absorbed. And if the *Sister Swan* was being absorbed . . . then so was the *Hooded Swan*. So was I. My spacesuit was being eaten, very slowly.

I made my way to the anterior wall of the loading bay, where the radiance shone just as brightly. There was a hatch that ought to be sealed. . . .

It wasn't.

It was buckled and torn. There was a crack between the edge of the hatch and the wall where it was supposed to be. I put my eye to the crack and I could see the silver light in the corridor of the ship, gently possessing every inch of the wall.

I moved back from the hatch. I didn't want to open it. I didn't want to go on. I put out a hand to touch the metal, and felt it yield.

I floated free, the reaction to my movement pushing me up into the empty volume of the bay. I was turning slowly on a vertical axis, coming around to face the mouth of hell through which I had come.

And I saw, framed in that mouth, a creature of pure white light . . . a thing with waving limbs that was spiraling counterclockwise and coming toward me. . . .

The power-gun was gripped firmly in my right hand. I had squirted just twice, on the lowest setting, to move me around in the bay. Now every instinct screamed inside me, telling me to raise the gun, open the power-control, and blast this shining thing out of existence.

The recoil would have thrown me clean through that

crumbling wall behind me, but my instinctive fears weren't
going to take note of a little thing like that.

I might have fired at what I saw, momentarily, as a
monster of white fire. The dagger of shock that sliced
through me might have convulsed my finger on the trigger.
But I have never been one to put my faith and fortune
into the beam of a gun. I have never liked shooting things.
I stopped myself firing, controlling the cruelest of my reflexes.

It was not until afterward that I realized the truth. The
being of white fire was a man in a spacesuit. It was . . . it
had to be . . . Nick delArco.

Alive.

He was floating toward me slowly. We collided with a
soft bump. He was wearing a filtered visor like mine and
I couldn't see his face at all through the glare and the dark
plastic. I tried to say something while our helmets were
touching, but the moment was quickly past.

He was clumsy. I knew he wasn't used to no-gee, and I
suspected that he was afraid of deep space. When we'd
had to cross over between ships in the Leucifer system he'd
shown signs of panic. I remembered, also, the crater where
the *Lost Star* was down, where I'd abandoned him in the
metamorphic jungle. He'd been scared then—petrified. I
had some idea of the effort and the courage that must have
been required to make him come out onto the skin of the
wrecked ship, at the mercy of the colored chaos.

Why?

I had to grapple with him to try to stabilize us within
the loading bay, but he didn't know what was required
and we kept floating about, spinning and bumping the
walls. I hoped fervently that I wouldn't be cutting across
any jagged edges. Theoretically, the suit shouldn't rip, but
there might be more than one reason why no one ever
takes them back to the store to complain.

Finally, I got him steady, and I forced the helmets together.

"Not that way," I heard him croak. "Round . . . the
airlock . . . air up front . . . losing it . . . leakage . . . came
to warn you."

He was in agony of some kind. Pain, or fear, or just
the legacy of hardship.

I pieced it together in my mind. The *Sister Swan* had

blown her hind end, and one of the air-traps in the body of the ship had sealed tight, cutting off the front end of the ship as a life-support unit. As time went by, the corrosion had begun, and the air-seal had begun to suffer. If I'd tried to go up into the belly of the ship through the loading-bay hatch I'd have reached the seal and found my way blocked. I wouldn't be able to open the hatch no matter what I did, but one tug, or a couple of taps, with the metal flaking and crumbling as it was, might have made the leak worse . . . maybe deadly. Nick and Eve—if they were both alive—couldn't have much in hand of the grim reaper. Their survival margin all along the line must have been pretty damn slim. It looked like I had arrived at the eleventh hour. Nick must have caught the vibration when the torpedo jarred the bulkhead—he could hardly have missed it. He must have guessed what it was, and come out to find me.

"It's OK, Nick," I said. My voice grated and slurred. "Take it easy," I added.

Together, with a measure of cooperation, we managed to get out onto the skin of the ship, and make our way ponderously over to the lock. It wasn't until I was actually into the lock that I realized just how much the war inside my head had sapped my strength, and just how weak Nick delArco was. There was a gee-field in the lock and the moment we hit it we sagged like a couple of sacks of potatoes. I could hardly move my hand to flood the lock with air, and I needed every second of the respite it gave me to recover myself enough to turn the wheel that would loose us into the ship.

When the pressure was finally equalized and the sealing bond broken, I was about ready to black out. The drug that had washed through my body all the while I was outside and helped me to survive now seemed to be turning bad, making me sick and dizzy. I was on the brink of collapse, spiritually as well as physically.

I felt myself burst into tears. There was a sickness inside my head which I somehow could not contain. I managed to close the inner hatch of the lock behind me, putting a double sheet of four-inch steel between our feeble selves and the prismatic inferno outside. I began to take off my helmet. Nick already had his off. He looked like something six weeks dead. His face was pasty gray, his hair was a ragged mess, his eyes were big and staring, as though he were in the grip of a high fever.

I fell into a black silence, but I was not allowed to remain there. Seconds later . . . I think it was only seconds later . . . I felt my face being slapped. I had to bring myself back up from the depths.

Nick had removed my helmet, and he was kneeling in the corridor, his body half supported by the wall, with my head in his lap, batting my face.

"Stop it," I said

"There's no time," he told me. His voice was thin and high pitched. His throat was dry.

"Stim-shot," I said. "In the control room."

He got the message. He helped me get up. I'm not sure whether he was carrying me or whether we were propping one another up. Somehow we made it to the control room. I was consummately grateful for the lateral gee-field in the body of the ship. If it had been vertical I think we might have never made it. We could have been stuck at the bottom of the ladder for good and all.

With my veins full of up-time and my gut full of anti-queasy I felt a hundred percent better and ready to face the world. It was strictly borrowed time but there was nowhere else I was going to get time except on high interest loan, and you can't choose your terms. Nick didn't look in shape to take too much artificial stimulation, so I gave him a modest dose of liquid moral support and hoped it would get him by.

"I don't think there's any of me left," I murmured.

"I thought for a moment you were dying," he said.

"You weren't the only one."

I sat up, and looked around me. The control room was dimly lit. The air was slightly over-warm and I could taste the fact that it was no longer perfect mixture. The *Sister Swan* was straining her resources. Nick and I were both on the floor, supported by the acceleration couches. I tried to haul myself up, but I couldn't. There was something missing, but for the moment I couldn't put my finger on it.

"Keep still," advised Nick.

"There's no time," I said.

"It's running out," he agreed, "but take a rest. Minutes."

Suddenly, I remembered the wind. I couldn't sense the

wind. He wasn't dead—I was sure of that—but I couldn't feel him. I wasn't aware of his presence. He was hurt.

Hey? I said, trying to elicit a response. None came. For the first time, he didn't respond. I felt suddenly alone, suddenly cut off. But I was sure he wasn't dead.

Nick was smiling. He was looking at me with big bug eyes, staring out of a hollow face, and he was beaming like a kid with a lollipop. I could see, welling up inside him, all the exultancy and the sheer sense of victory. It was breaking out of him in that vast smile.

"Did it ever occur to you," I whispered, trying to sound friendly, "how bloody useless you are?"

He thought I didn't mean it. Perhaps I didn't. The grin stayed and I couldn't help smiling back, just a little.

"I thought you'd come," he said.

"You presume one hell of a lot," I said, "on the basis of a short, slight friendship. One hell of a lot."

"It was in the cards," he said.

"Some bastard's dealing out of a crooked deck," I told him. "Do you reckon to spend the rest of your life sitting on your fat rump in the middle of sick space waiting for me to come and pull you out?"

"These things happen," he said. The smile was fading. There was some bite in what I said.

"Too bloody often," I said. "And always to us."

"Twice," he said.

"Too bloody often," I repeated.

"How long were you out there?" he asked.

"I don't know."

"You felt it?"

"Felt it? Man, you have no idea."

"It gets into you," he said. "It gets into you and you can't get it out. It's worse, out there?"

"Much worse," I confirmed.

"But you made it."

"Halfway."

He nodded. "I rigged a sled," he said. "I knew you'd come. Time on my hands. I rigged a sled to carry her."

I remembered what was missing then.

"Where is she?" I asked, my voice suddenly turning harsh. I felt about ready to stand up now. The drugs had settled down. I was almost back to human shape.

"Right over there," he said, pointing to the cradle. I

didn't follow the direction with his finger. I was looking
into his face. His eyes had a cold intensity I didn't like.
His jaw was set hard. Dilute though my feelings were, they
were stirring again.

"She's not dead," he said, misreading what was in my
face.

"Hurt bad?" I asked.

He nodded slightly, then seemed to change his mind and
made as if to shake his head.

"She's hurt," he said. "In the head. Inside. When we
came through . . . she tried . . . I'll swear she did all she
could . . . you already saw the blown-out cannon. The
chamber cracked. You saw it all . . . you know better than
I do . . . but she did all she could. Inside the hood . . .
something happened. She's alive, but . . . "

I understood. Intuitively, I could follow the argument.
I knew what had happened. She was living the ship. The
ship's body was hers. When the cannon blew, it was a
part of herself exploding. When the flux bled, it was her
body that was bleeding. She was right inside Rothgar when
the flux roasted him, right inside the *Sister Swan* when she
died. . . .

"Comatose," Nick was saying, "maybe catatonic. I don't
know. I daren't move her from the cradle. I've hooked
her up to intravenous. But she doesn't wake up. I think . . .
when the ship went out . . . she just went out with it."

"I know," I said.

"When we get her back," he said, "it'll be OK. If anyone can help her, it's Charlot."

I felt like laughing, but I couldn't let the bitterness spill
over like that. I had to take it easy, for the time being.

"Don't bet on it," I said quietly. "Don't count my
chickens. There's nothing in the rules says the books have
to balance at the end. This isn't the movies. There's a lot
of if between here and home. This is *it*, you see, friend.
This is what I always tried to get into your thick skull.
People die. People get hurt. You knew the score before
you started and you didn't want to believe it. You always
knew the odds and it's no good trying to bend them now.
There may always be some idiot to come and pull you out,
while there are idiots like me. But nobody has a God-
given right to win, Nick. There isn't an answer to every
problem. You *can't* just pencil in the next miracle and

wait for it. It doesn't work that way. If anyone can help her, it's Charlot. Sure, Nick, sure. Do you want me to tell you how many kinds of fool you have to be to think that that's an *answer?*"

"No," he said.

I got up, and I walked around the cradle, to look into it. The light was coming from behind, so the cradle was in shadow. Eve's face looked placid—stony calm. She didn't look dead but she was stiller than in sleep. Her face was warm . . . she looked less like a ghost than Nick did. But there was a hardness—the bone structure seemed to be carved out of rock.

I reached out a hand and touched her forehead with my fingertips. I could feel a slight pulse at the side. She was real, though she hardly looked it, sheltered by the shadow.

My mind slid right back through time, quickly riffling through the pages of my past. I ended up at the moment when I'd taken her brother's corpse out of the wreck of the *Javelin*. It wasn't the faces that linked the moments— Lapthorn had lost his face in the crash and there had been nothing left of him that wasn't smashed. It wasn't the faces, but the feeling. The ghost of Lapthorn's memory passed out of Eve at that moment, just as Lapthorn's life had passed out of his body. Eve became Eve, in my eyes. No one else.

I never loved Michael Lapthorn. I never even liked him much. He existed for me, and as a part of me, in my eyes. He was never a person. He was like the ship—an instrument, a lever. A hand or a bone. Not real, in himself. I'd made Eve into a relic—the bone of the hand, the charred end of the bone. Somewhere, on a world whose name I can't remember, Lapthorn had lost a hand. An alien wore it as a talisman now. I'd worn the rest of Lapthorn just as the alien had worn that hand. I'd never been able to disconnect Eve from her brother's memory. Not until now.

I recognized Eve, for the first time.

Nick was watching me. He was saying nothing.

—Grainger. Listen.

A thin whisper, coming from deep within.

Leave me alone, I said. I felt a faint flush of shame after I'd said it. It had been pure reflex. I didn't mean it. But there were so many things that needed thinking about and they kept piling up.

Give me time, I said to him.

—How much have we got? he asked. I felt his sense of urgency.

"We have to move," said Nick. "The ship . . . it can't hold much longer. We have to get away. We have to go back."

I returned my attention to him.

"You know what it's like out there?" I asked.

"The colors—getting into your mind."

"That's it," I said. "When we go out, it'll come at you. You have to resist it. You think you can do it?"

"What choice have I got?"

"The *Hooded Swan*'s hurt too," I told him. "Most of her sensors are out or marginal. The nerve-net took a pounding. My crew is trying to fix it all up, but they can only go so far. The ship is way beyond their experience. They never saw anything like it before."

Nick looked faintly puzzled. "Johnny?" he said.

I shook my head. "Not with us," I told him. I didn't explain. "What I want to know," I continued, "is whether you can fix us up so we can fly?"

He spread his palms wide. "Whatever can be done," he said. "I can do it."

"Fair enough," I said. "It'll put an end to your uselessness. For once."

"Thanks a lot," he said.

"Don't take it to heart," I said. "I'm only mean because I'm hurt."

"It's OK," he said.

"This sled you mentioned," I went on. "What is it? Will it carry the three of us?"

He nodded.

"Well then," I said. "There's no more to it, is there? Let's go."

He shook his head. "You need rest," he said. "And we both need something more than what we have floating around inside us to help us get across."

He was right. If we tried to cross back now I'd be running my neck into a noose. You can't keep moving forever. Sometimes you have to stop. But did we even have time to slow down?

"How much time have we in hand?" I asked him.

"Enough," he said. I had a nasty suspicion that he was trading on hope again, putting his trust in the symmetry of events and the knowledge that the U.S. Cavalry always charges in at the last minute no matter how desperate things are. But I had to accept what he said.

"Let's eat," he said.

It was a good idea. I wasn't hungry, but it would give us both something to think about. We needed some activity to occupy our minds.

I went with him to the galley. While we got things ready I watched him, covertly but closely. He was bearing up well. He was pale and untidy and tired, but he was still operating and still in balance. I wondered how much the crash had hurt *him*, and how much the mind-eating force outside had been able to do to him through the walls of the ship. I concluded that he was OK. He'd taken it all so far, and he could take some more.

I took time out to come back to the wind.

Are you OK, I asked him.

—No I'm not, he replied.

How bad?

—I can't tell. No standard for measurement.

I'm sorry.

—So am I.

Don't worry, I told him. We made it once. We can make it again. This time you know it can be done. You can take it and win. It can't kill you.

—It's not as simple as that, he told me.

It never is, I assured him. You just have to pretend.

—You don't understand, he said.

No, I admitted.

—I don't think I'm going to come through this, he said. I think I'm going to die.

I tried, I said. I really did try. But I can't help you. There's just no way.

—I know, he said. We have to fight it independently. It's the only chance *you* have. You can come through. I can't.

You have everything I have, I pointed out. You have the talent and the know-how to use it. You can pull through.

—You've got to believe me, he insisted.

Why?

—I want you to listen to me. I want you to take what I have to give you.

I sensed a dirty trick. All my old fears marched back in their serried ranks. All my old, never-dead prejudices welled up inside me.

No fusion, I said. I'm sorry, but I'm not going to merge my mind with yours. It's no matter whether I believe you or not. You know I can't and won't accept it.

—It's not that, he said. It wouldn't work that way. We'd both be destroyed if we tried any trick like that. It wouldn't make me safe to fade into you—it would just make you vulnerable. That's not what I want. Can you believe me, Grainger, when I say that the most important thing to me right now is that *you* should get out of this alive and in one piece? Can you accept that?

Maybe, I said. I see how that might be.

—It is, he said. I think I'm going to die, but you can pull through. You mean a lot to me. Grainger . . . I suppose that sounds ridiculous. I know you never wanted me, always wanted to be rid of me, always resented me, maybe hated me. But I'm not just a parasite and you're not just a vehicle. Can you accept *that*?

Get to the point, I said.

—You could get your way, he said. It takes a real double deal, but you could get your way. I didn't think it was possible, until now. But you could get out of here without me. I just want you to do me a favor.

What?

—Remember me.

I will, I told him. Believe me, I'll remember you all my days.

But that wasn't what he meant, and I knew it. He meant a good deal more than that. He wanted to leave something with me to remember him by.

—I want you to know about me, he said. That's all. I just want you to know who and what I am. I want you to understand. I don't want to tip my memories or my knowledge or even my talents into your brain like a load of coal. It's too dangerous anyhow, at this stage. I don't want you to accept any of me into yourself. But I do want you to know. I want to *tell* you. About me. All the things you never wanted to hear. All the things that you thought might make me into a living being instead of a voice in your skull. I only want you to know who I am. That's all.

You know damn well that if you talk I haven't any choice but to listen, I told him.

—You have the choice, he said. I'm giving you the choice. Without the choice, what would it be worth? You know what I'm asking you, Grainger. I'm asking you not to let me die faceless. Don't make me die a nothing, an empty voice inside your head, like a disease or some kind of insanity. Just let me be what I am, that's all.

I didn't know what to do. I didn't seem to be in touch with the way things were moving. I could understand what he wanted, just about. He wanted me to admit to being his friend. He didn't want to die while the only man who knew he existed hated him like poison. I think that makes sense.

But I didn't want to know. I never had. I did resent him. I did hate him. Those are simple facts.

Nick and I finished eating. He looked at me expectantly.

"I want to lie down," I said. "Just a few minutes. I'll be OK. It's just a matter of getting ready. You get the sled mounted for the eject. I'll help you with Eve, if you can put a suit on her. OK?"

He nodded. I went back to the control room, and I lay down on one of the couches. I didn't cast a glance toward the cradle. I shut my eyes.

I could feel something like a thin veil choking my thoughts. Even in here—even in the womb of reality—we weren't totally free. There was still an alien existence, still a force searching in my mind. It was trying to corrode me as it had corroded the ship, trying to absorb me into a mode of existence I was never born to experience. It was very faint, its touch was cobweb-light, but I was nevertheless aware of the vast power behind the touch. I was still aware that I was an unbelievably tiny particle somehow lost from my own cosmos, negligible in another.

I knew how terribly alone I might be if it were not for the apparitions of flesh which were my fellow particles.

And their voices. . . .

Go ahead, I said with my inner voice. I'm listening.

XVII

—I have no name. One of my hosts was named Celtis, another Gyr, but those names were no more mine than yours. I might have named myself, had I been introduced to humankind earlier in my existence, but among the Gallacellans names are not so important, and on the world where my life began there was no such thing as a name. There was never a need for such a thing. My kind do not meet face-to-face with separate faces which need to be identified. We possess no shape, no form to be labeled. We live within. What we have, and what we are, we share. We do not isolate ourselves from everything around us. We are *where* we are as much as we are who and what are. We do not perceive ourselves as *things*, to be told apart from other things by naming. With you, I know, it is a little different. But I came to you on the wind, and you think of me still as a wind that talked, not as a being that was only a part of the wind.

—I am a pattern. That is all. In a sense, there is no being of any kind who is anything more than a pattern, but most things are crystallized, fixed patterns. I have ubiquity. My patterning is not unique. You are a pattern *of* something—of electrical impulses in a material matrix. I am a pattern *in* something, a traveling pattern. In one phase, I may be molecules of a gas. When the gas is inhaled, the pattern may infect molecules in blood, electrical impulses in brain. When my pattern is a mimic in inert matter, I myself am inert. When it is a mimic in a thinking system, I think. The transfer of my pattern from one medium to another cannot be consciously controlled. A natural tropism carries me always into the most useful and sophisticated medium, and once I am metamorphosed from dormancy to self-awareness the only way out of the matrix is death . . .

the death of the host. When the host-pattern breaks down, there is no recourse for the mimic but to be recoded. Into matter, into liquid or gas. Eventually, there is reinfection.

—You were a castaway on the world which you named Lapthorn's Grave. I was a castaway not once but twice. My host was stranded on that world. When he died, I was stranded again . . . I became a cloud, eventually—a whisper traveling on the wind. I may have explored every inch of that bleak rock ten times or a thousand times. I have no way of knowing. I could have become a seed inside the Gallacellan's skull, initially—hopefully waiting to be devoured. I might have entered into the organization of a bacterium or a protozoan, for a brief while. You see, perhaps you can begin to understand, how little I can know myself.

—I am an entity, of a kind. Not your kind, I know. You have called me alien, though as I am now, in your mind, I am quite human. I am exactly as human as you, and no more. I am too perfect a mimic to be anything else. You have called me a parasite, although I have borrowed nothing from you that leaves you any poorer. I have stolen the image of your mind, like a camera, but you know that the camera does not steal the soul with the image. I have lived in you, and the energy by which my life is fueled has been borrowed from your substance. But I have paid for this in kind. I have gathered energy for you and in you. I have allowed you to make better use of your own physiological resources. I may well leave you better than I found you, for some of what I have taught your body will be permanently imprinted. You will be fitter, healthier. I have given you life itself, in some small measure, in return for the life you have given me. This is over and above the conscious help I have given you, for which you owe me nothing. I am *not* alien. I am not a parasite. I can be human or Khormon or any of a million kinds of being which you will never meet. *None* of these beings is alien to me. I know no such thing as an alien being, or I knew none such until we came into this universe. Perhaps even here there are no aliens. Perhaps what I perceive as death here is only another transformation. Perhaps something that *was* me, something perhaps not *wholly* changed, can live on—a commensal in a universal mind. Perhaps there *are* no aliens.

—My world, of course, had no name. Its people had no names nor did its animals and plants. In time, if evolution had taken a particular line other than the one it did, the people of my world might have been what you call men, or humanoids. They might have become beings like you, sealed into cages of matter. But chance dictated otherwise. Chance, or the law behind chance which we cannot envisage.

—Your brain is packaged by its skull, but a skull is not necessarily a cage. There are means of unlocking the cage, means of transcending the isolation. On my world, there are creatures of body and creatures of mind. We are not alike, but we do not draw lines between ourselves, cutting out boundaries and making skulls into fortresses. *That is not the only way*. Mind, on my world, is something shared, not something *owned*. We do not have secret hoards which we call ourselves. We are not what you would call a group mind. To speak of *one* mind or *many* is, in a way, nonsense. Body is singular. Mind is not. Only the singular can become plural.

—You would think of my world as a hell, I think. You might not be able to define the difference between my world and this alien continuum which threatens your mind. You would see the forces alive in my world as destructive ones, though they are not. I only wish I could show you the difference, but I don't know if you can understand even what I have said already. I can only use your concepts, and they do not stretch very far. But this, I think, you can see: that what you think of as alien, you yourself have made alien. Here, now, you are exposed to the truly alien. Can you not use this experience to realign your own ideas? In the real universe, the alien is in your eyes and in your mind. It is not in the way things *are*.

—I have been a wanderer. An explorer. A searcher. I wish that I could have returned to my own world, ultimately, to take my explorations back home. That is where they belong. I know that you would never have consented to take me home, and perhaps no human host would have done. When your kind find out about my world they will want to destroy it, obliterate it completely from the face of existence. You will see it as a danger. I will not tell even you where to find my world, even though it would serve no purpose for you to tell anyone else, and there would be no point in anyone else destroying it. As you know from Titus Charlot, what can exist, will exist, and nothing you can do will alter that. Titus Charlot, of course, might find in the existence of my world and beings like me the ultimate goal which he hopes to contribute toward—the unity of sentient life, and the unity of knowledge and ideas and creativity and feeling. But he would not want it our way. He wants it his own way, through history. He believes in history. I don't think I do. I know that you don't. But our nonbelief extends in two different directions.

—I came from my world by my own free will. It was not an accident. I was not commanded. I fragmented myself and I came away, a passenger in a tiny cage. You cannot imagine the kind of loneliness which I have felt, in the vast depths of your inner space. Outer space, what you call "deep" space . . . that is nothing . . . but inside, there is isolation and darkness. You have always thought of me in terms of threat and control. You have feared that I would "take over." That could not be. There was no way. A fusion . . . a sharing . . . a communion . . . I could have wished for something of this kind. Perhaps that, too, could not be. I have felt that it might be so, that there is nothing in your universe but loneliness. I hope and I believe that I am wrong.

—I know myself, and therefore you, rather less than you do. You may have answers where I can only suggest questions. I have always tried to give you answers, but you have never accepted them. I think you were right.

—You will never tell anyone about me. You never have —you feel that you cannot, that there is something which makes me unreal relative to the things which you perceive as real. No one would believe in me. I think you are right in this, also. I don't think you can or should explain. I don't think there is any way that you could explain me. If you tried, they would make you an alien. They would call you mad. They would send you to an alienist, for diagnosis and therapy. Do you see me as they do? Do you think of yourself as mad? I don't think so. You know the difference.

—I hope that you're able to listen to all this, Grainger, though I'm not sure that you can. Perhaps it doesn't matter, to you. Perhaps it shouldn't matter to me. Is this the real me, or is it the human me? But there's no difference. Not really.

—I think you still hate me, Grainger. I don't think there's any other way, for you. I love you . . . there's no other way for me. I don't want to give you any advice. I don't want to tell you any secrets. I don't want to make you take anything you don't want to take. But I'd like you to listen. I want you to remember me as something that I am, not just something you think I am—some excuse you've made up for me, some name you can give me and confine me with. Do you see? Do you see, through the confusion and the wandering, what I'm trying to put into your mind? Some idea of me. Some grain of an attitude by which you can look at me and *see* me.

—Think of me. Think *about* me.

—Perhaps that says it all. I don't know what else I can add. How do you put yourself into words in a matter of minutes? You know all the rest. You know that if I do die you'll have to get along without me—play your own panpipes and talk your own Gallacellan. You know that there may come a time when you'll wish I was with you. I don't have to remind you of that. You know that it's going to be a little bit harder, maybe inside as well as out. But still you'll be happy, because right now and until I die, you hate me. That's life.

—Isn't it?

XVIII

It's not all hate.

That's all I had to say. That's all I had to tell him. What else was there?

In any case, we were in a hurry. We got Eve onto the middle of the sled, and with one of us on either side she was as secure as it was possible to keep her. How secure her mind would be we couldn't know. In all probability, the coma was her best possible defense against the possibility of invasion and destruction, but it might work the other way and render her all the more vulnerable. We couldn't do anything about that, except hope.

Nick and I were both drugged up. We were both slow and euphorically calm. We didn't dare shoot anything like that into Eve.

In any case, we were all in the arms of fortune. It wasn't courage or genius which had brought me to the *Sister Swan* and it wasn't those things which would take the three of us back. We went forth into the inferno, and fired the jets, pointed our nose at the star in the sky, and hoped.

We didn't know how long the journey would take, or even whether real time was of any significance here.

As before, the assault took time to build up, but it kept on building. I felt it clamp itself into my skull like something wet and sticky. I felt it permeating my brain.

This time, I was oddly detached. I was aware of what was happening and I knew what was going to happen. Having played the game before I knew the shape of it, the way it would be won, and the probable result. I was reliving rather than living. It was as though the outward journey had provided me with a corridor of retreat. I was confident, this time, that I could get through. I was able to observe and monitor my own thoughts and reactions.

I was confident on the wind's behalf too. Somehow, I felt he was going to make it.

The aspect of the incredible continuum was no longer frightening in itself. The invasion of my mind by its emphatic forces was repulsive, but not horrifying. My reaction was not extreme. I did not contribute so much myself to the distortion of perception. I yielded none of my sanity.

Whether this was entirely a good thing I can never be sure. Had it not been for my preparedness, my confidence, I would never have begun to sense even a glimmer of order in the chaos. I knew that to discover some sense in it was dangerous, but I could not help myself. Somehow, I was no longer so utterly remote, so entirely locked up in myself. I was able to feel that there was being behind it all, that on its own terms, this universe was just as real and sane as our own. Its spatiotemporal fabric might be horribly twisted from our point of view, but it had its own neatness and rigidity and regulation. The appreciation which I achieved of the ordination of the alternate continuum was aesthetic rather than intellectual, but even so, I did find a way to see it.

The wind knew what I knew, and saw as I saw, and I realized why he had been so certain that he wouldn't make it. It was not chaos that he was afraid of, but himself, and with good reason. He saw, and he understood. He was made to adapt and understand. Where I could begin to divine the shape of space and the orientation of time he could go all the way, and never come back.

—Shut your eyes, he said. His voice twanged in my skull like a guitar string. It was horribly distorted.

I shut my eyes, but only for a moment. I dared not cut myself off from sight more than momentarily. I wanted to keep my attention fixed on the single star. I wanted to be secure in the knowledge that we weren't going to miss it, that we *couldn't* miss it.

Shutting my eyes would have made no difference. Not to him. The fog that glittered on my visor obscured my vision enough to render the colors impotent, if they could be so rendered. I couldn't see much except the star, and the force which was invading me wasn't going to go away just because I closed my eyes.

He knew that, too. He left me alone, to focus myself

on the *Hooded Swan*. He didn't interfere with my battle, and he fought his own as well as he could. I managed to stay calm and isolated, cut off from everything, including the wind. He withdrew. I couldn't feel him.

Time passed, but the star remained still and tiny in the sky. It didn't grow. The outward passage had seemed fast —a plunge into a pool of light. This time it felt slow— very slow. The difference might have been in the feeling, but I don't think so. It was the "current"—the distortion of distance. The journey began, but it did not seem to proceed. I realized, eventually, that I was waiting, that nothing was happening, that the moment was stretching and might stretch forever.

I wondered what poor Nick was feeling, first time out. Maybe it wasn't the same for him. Maybe he was living the time all compressed into a long scream, packaged and collapsed, as I had on the outward run. I never asked him.

The force was closed in on my mind. I could feel it hanging in me. It didn't feel much of a threat, suspended in time as I was. I could feel the balance of the drug and the inconstant insistence that I wake beyond consciousness, but the balance seemed weighted to prostration, immovable. There was no straining, no teetering, no possibility of breakdown and cataclysm. The forces were immense, but passive. The stress on me—the fulcrum—was smothering, but not strangling.

I had the odd sensation that time was draining through me like grains of sand through the waist of an hourglass, but the fall of the grains was so slow and graceful, as though there were hardly any gravity to pull them through.

The waiting went on, and the only pressure which built up was the pressure of wondering what I might be waiting *for*.

The star grew no nearer in the incoherent sky.

Time rolled on like an ocean swell, and my own sense of time seemed to elongate, to synchronize with the lethargic quality of indigenous time. I felt that I was wrapped around the universe instead of it around me, and that I was squashing it, molding its natural laws with my tough fingers, making it over into a shape I knew.

As this strange consciousness grew, I seemed to feel the alien continuum begin to wriggle within my grip, like a great ponderous eel.

The equilibrium remained undisturbed, but its dynamism grew as I grew to the scale of events. I felt healthy, alive, excited, although I was conscious in the back of my mind that this was no less losing the battle than the horrific hunted, violated feeling which had possessed me on the way in. The weightiness of the balanced sides was lost, and the whole idea of myself as fulcrum was lost with it.

Slowly, alien consciousness crept up on me. It didn't come steadily, and it was slow, but it built up. Little by little, I began to arrange analogies. I discovered a way to think about shape, about the kind of organization, about the kind of pattern involved. I was reaching out to the force. I was being drawn, dragged, an iron filing to a magnet or a moth to a flame. I could not help myself. I was realigning myself, reintegrating myself, reunderstanding myself, reinterpreting myself.

I was aware of the being . . .

. . . and of the *mind*.

The model which I formed was not an image, in the visual sense, nor was it a shape delineated by touch. It was a purely intellectual sensation of how things related to one another in this continuum.

I no longer have the model. I could not retain it once I was beyond the reach of the forces which sustained it. I can remember it, but I cannot reconstruct it. My knowledge of the return to the *Hooded Swan* and what happened en route is woefully imperfect. Sometimes I used to wake from a dream knowing that in the dream I saw or knew something that was original and important, but which totally eluded my waking brain. I now stand in the same position with respect to this particular experience of the alien universe. Even now, when I emerge from a torpor induced by drink or drugs, I am occasionally left with a feeling that I have been away into the farther realms of my imagination—into territory which I cannot re-explore while transfixed by the certainty of consciousness.

I no longer have at my disposal all that I learned during my second journey through the pavonian gulf, and the account which I have to give can only be rendered in peripheral terms. I have neither adequate language nor adequate imagination. All that I am sure of is the truth.

The being did not speak to me. We did not communicate, in that way, but we were linked for a while—a long while, I believe, although the passage of time was probably quite irrelevant. I discovered the being and it discovered me. We observed one another.

There was a third participant in the observation—the wind. It is not impossible that the wind acted as a kind of catalyst in allowing me to perceive as much as I did without injury. Perhaps all I really received was the backwash of his own observations, a filtered echo. I don't know. I can't ask the wind.

The wind was destroyed.

He was a victim of Heisenberg's Uncertainty Principle—sometimes the act of observation alters the properties of both observed and observer. The wind was altered . . . perhaps the cosmic mind also. The one may have been killed, the other . . . who can tell? Perhaps, in some way, the wind still lives beyond the Nightingale lens—a parasite, within a wholly different kind of organism.

This is the truth that I learned:

Titus Charlot was only half right, if that. Beyond the Nightingale Nebula there is no other universe—not the kind of other universe he was trying to find, at any rate. The seam in space which is the core of the Nightingale lesion delineates a body not actually *in* our universe, but by no means independent of it. It may be regarded as being *in* another universe because it is not in ours, or it may be regarded as a universe in its own right, but it is certainly not infinite. I do not think that the *where* of the problem is important at all. I think that the organism is independent of *where* and *when*—it is so very different in terms of *what* it is that the subsidiary questions lose their meaning. Space, time, and being are inextricably bound up with one another. Difference of any kind is difference of all kinds.

The organism is a parasite upon the energy-properties of space. By maintaining a coexistent but not continuous relationship with the universe it manages to sustain its own energy-system in profiting from the laws which determine the organization of ours. In brief, it is a *sac* in space into which energy naturally drains. The rate of flow is very tiny, but enough differential exists between the energy-states to assure that a tiny flow is by no means insignificant. It is not the stealing of a little diffuse starlight or the small energy of spatial distortion which sustains the organism, but the different laws of physics which apply to its internal organization.

The fact does remain, however, that the organism is very slowly eating the galaxy.

Erg by erg, our entire system of being is dying, draining into the mouth of the Nightingale. I think it almost certain there are other mouths like it, if not in our own galaxy, in others. Incalculable aeons will pass before the Nightingale consumes as much energy as it takes to sustain one man's existence through one small lifetime, but the one man surrenders all the energy in the end—all is recycled courtesy of entropy—while the Nightingale does not.

In all probability, the Nightingale is growing. Over a billion years or so the mouth may gape a little wider, the body surrender less of what impinges upon the lens. Perhaps, as it grows hungry, the organism will migrate toward the galactic core. If there are more of these beings to be found, that is where to look for them—in the core. They might dine more richly there.

Perhaps the organism will divide. Perhaps, in time (aeonic time, not negligible millennia) the destiny of the galaxy is to feed a plague of such creatures, a population explosion of cosmic parasites. They may divide every few billion years or so, in exponential series. No one can know. Even Titus Charlot could not catch the merest glimpse of such possibilities in his imagination.

The Nightingale might someday be renamed. It might come to be called the Hookworm or the Lamprey. But there is no real need. On our scale of being, the thing we are aware of will always be the song. The organism may be eating our universe but it means nothing in human terms. Nothing at all. It cannot interfere with human life, unless we persist in throwing starships into its mouth. And even then . . . there are means of escape. The Nightingale operates on a scale which is beyond our imagination, let alone our understanding. With the full power of our inner vision we can only *suggest* that such a thing exists. We can only describe it in our own feeble terms. There is no meaningful way that we can share the stage of existence with the Nightingale.

We have the song, and that is all.

It does not matter to us whether it is the swan song of the galaxy.

How long I spent in the limbo of existence, while my mind touched the mind of the being in whom we floated, I could not tell. The chronometer aboard the *Hooded Swan* could give us no reliable estimation.

I know, however, that we did reach the ship, in the end. I survived, and so did Nick delArco. No one can claim any credit for that fact—it was not our doing, nor was it the wind. It was the way the cards happened to fall. Heroism and justice had nothing to do with it. We survived, and that is all. Our identities remained intact and . . . we believe . . . unchanged.

We reached the *Hooded Swan* and abandoned the sled. We maneuvered ourselves, and Eve's inert body, into the airlock. We passed through into the relative haven of the ship's interior.

Inside the hull all was still and silent. The lighting was dim. Sam and Mina must have been aware of our arrival, but they did not come to meet us. As soon as I removed my helmet I could feel that something was wrong.

I called out, taking some pleasure from the substantial sound of my voice in the air. Mina came out of one of the cabins. She looked haggard and ghost-ridden. When I left, she had looked exhausted, physically and spiritually, but now she was torn as well. Hurt by long waiting and loss of hope and the agony of despair. I glanced sideways at Nick, who seemed to have shrunk visibly since we set out from the *Sister Swan*. His complexion looked like porcelain, and his whole bearing was that of a puppet on lax strings.

"I gave you up," she said. "It's been so long."

I moved forward and took her by the arm. I was tempted to shake her, to try to jerk some life back into her, but I dared not. She seemed so fragile.

"What about the drive-unit?" I asked gently. "The works. Is it finished?"

She gave me the strangest look, as if I were mad, as if the question I'd asked was meaningless, impossible.

She began to cry. She didn't sob, she didn't even bow her head. The tears just rolled out of the corners of her eyes. There was no immediate emotional shock. I still held her upright, fearing that if I let her go she would crumple like a doll.

Behind me, Nick sat down on the floor, his head against

the bulkhead. He looked clean out of his mind, too tired even to occupy his own senses. He was holding Eve's hand . . . she was stretched out like a corpse.

"Where's Sam?" I asked gently.

She raised her own hands then, and gripped me by the shoulders, lowering her head onto my chest. I eased her upright again, waiting for an answer.

I had to repeat the question.

Finally, she said, "In there."

She meant the cabin from which she'd come. My eyes traveled beyond her, looking into the darkness behind the open door, but I couldn't see him.

"What happened?" I demanded, my voice rising in spite of my determined self-control.

"He . . . " she began, and then changed her mind. "It just . . . "

She couldn't find a way to tell me.

"He's dead," I said, guessing wildly.

"No," she said, and then I knew. I knew what I ought to have suspected all along. I knew why I should have left Sam at home and brought Johnny. I knew what had given way.

"He's blind," she said, finally gathering the strength. "He can't see."

XIX

———◆———

"It just closed in on me," said Sam. "Came down like a curtain. For years, I knew . . . this was the way it had to go. Bit by bit, I lost the strength. The cones in the retina, just . . . burning out, I guess . . . it happens to a lot of men in the kind of space I've been flying all my life, It happens slowly. I didn't expect . . . this. I'm sorry. Truly sorry."

We'd gathered all the human debris in the control room. We'd pulled ourselves together, one way and another. Nick was sleeping—he'd need rest and recovery before he was in any fit condition to tackle the delicate work of rigging the sensors out in the nose and the wings. It wouldn't be a long job, but it would need all his strength and precision.

Mina's tears kept appearing in stops and starts. She didn't seem to me the kind of person who cried a lot, but she was past caring about appearances and she just didn't have any control over her lachrymal glands. I almost wished that I could make more use of the same outlet. My head felt so full that it could only benefit from having some of the pressure taken off. Sam was in good physical shape except for his eyes, but there was no way I could judge his true state of mind. With his eyesight had gone the whole foundation of his facial expression. The integrity of the behavior of his face had been lost. He was like a statue now, for the most part, with his face never reflecting or echoing anything that he said. When he smiled, he looked like a stranger.

"All I need," he said, "is the loan of a pair of eyes. Mina or Mr. delArco. Either. They can read the dials. They know what the numbers signify. They know how the drive works. I can move the levers, play the keys. I can do the work, if they'll only lend me their eyesight."

"You think you can do that?" I asked Mina.

"I'll try," she said.

"That's not what I asked."

"Maybe he can do it better," she said, pointing at Nick. "That's for you to decide. Somebody has to do it."

I shook my head.

She just stared at me. I wondered how I could show her, convince her that it was no good, that it couldn't work.

"Sam," I said, "stand up." He stood, and I faced him. I raised my fists into the air, so that both my forearms were vertical seven inches or so apart, one slightly higher than the other.

"Right, Sam," I said. "You're back on the *Sandman*. The phase-shift operator is on your left, the power-feed to the mass accelerator is on your right. Reach out and take the levers." He put up his hands, and after a moment or two of preliminary fumbling he gripped my wrists. "OK, Sam," I continued. "We're in free flight. Forget the lifting equipment and the cannons. We're making a couple of hundred in dead straight flight, and I'm taking her up from phase two to phase three in a couple of minutes. Just a transfer, no more. We're leaking ten, maybe twenty per from the drive same as we usually do. You're counting down and you're at fifty. Take the count, Sam."

He began counting, from fifty down. His eyes were open, staring straight ahead. The direction of his gaze just skimmed my hairline. I looked up into his face.

When he reached twenty I told him we were coming off-balance. At ten I told him the accelerator wasn't boosting the synchrotron enough. At five I told him the gap was getting critical. At minus two I told him we missed transfer and were bleeding forty-five per and increasing.

All the while I could feel his hands straining at the two fake levers. I could feel his hesitations, his uncertainties, his mistakes.

When it was all over and I told him to let go, his hands began shaking.

"I'm sorry," he said.

"It doesn't mean a thing," protested Mina.

"It would be exactly the same with the *Swan*'s drive," I said. "You've got to realize that Sam didn't learn to fly from the instruction book. He doesn't do it by the manual; he does it by feel. He becomes part of his machine. He doesn't *think* about what he's doing—he's not a computer who can just be reprogrammed to respond to a whole new set of signals and stimuli. If you stood behind him and told him what was on a dial, you wouldn't just be doing something for him that he'd normally do himself. Sam doesn't *read* the dials . . . when the dials move, so does he. He's a *part* of the whole system. He acts with it, not upon it. I'm sorry, Sam, but it's not just a matter of lending you a pair of eyes. It can't be done. We can't make an engineer out of someone peering over your shoulder. It's not on."

"Sorry," said Sam.

"Not your fault," I told him. "Mine."

"No," he said.

"I'm the captain of this ship," I told him. "I'm responsible for the crew. I knew your eyes were going the moment I clapped my own eyes on you. I took the risk. I lost. Not you."

There was a momentary silence.

"We're trapped," said Mina.

"It's not easy," I confirmed.

"What do we do?" asked Sam, sounding as if it didn't matter the least. They both had that kind of look about them.

"We sleep," I said. "We all need it. We recover ourselves, so far as we can. Then we attack the problem. Whatever we can do, we do. Wherever the best chance is, that's the way we take. Simple as that."

Simple it was, but as I said, it wasn't easy. The *Hooded Swan* was a great ship, but also she was by no means the kind of thing a kid of six could handle right off the bat. Where a man like Rothgar had failed to cope, any experienced and competent engineer could be in deep trouble. A dilettante would be a nonstarter. But when the choice lies between a blind man and a moron, who do you choose?

I needed sleep. I needed a revelation, a miraculous inspiration. I should have known that sleep was no place to go looking for it.

I made Mina and Sam go to their beds, and I went to mine. I had to take a shot, but even so I had bad dreams. In fact, I had nightmares.

There were ghostly voices inside my head. Echoes. My dreams were filled with weird images that weren't mine at all, but his. He wasn't there. He was dead. But all that earthly remains . . .

I'd never hear his voice again. The inside of my head

would be silent as the tomb during all my waking moments. But retreating into my subconscious, sagging back from my senses, I'd find his bleaching bones. The wreckage of a second mind. Memories. Shards. An immortal soul . . . ?

The cross that I had put upright on Lapthorn's grave refused to stay that way. I could have laid it down instead, laid it flat, or I could have thrown it away altogether. What did a cross mean to Lapthorn? Or to me? But no. The soil at the head of the grave was too shallow and too dry, but I kept standing that cross up and making it stay. Until the wind came and blew it down.

Why did I bother? I just don't know. It didn't mean a thing. Lapthorn had never been confined by that cross. He'd haunted me, one way or another. And now the wind . . . the wind who rode the wind who blew the cross down and down and down. . . . I couldn't get him out of my mind either. Not finally. Death couldn't free me. He could always come back to me, in my sleep. . . .

I saw his world, through alien eyes. I saw through Gallacellan eyes. Just glimpses of an infinity of possibilities. I saw through my own eyes, without my own mind. Frightening. I heard his words rattling in my brain, jumbled and threadless. I knew that all the words I heard weren't words he'd uttered in the past. He was still making new ones. There was more of him left than just my memories of him. Much more.

I was disturbed and afraid, that first time. Much later, it ceased to be a nightmare. A hundred journeys into the ruins of his mind made them familiar, easy to get into, not frightening at all. The first time, though, I was suffering from the aftereffects of far too much junk, from physical deterioration, maybe even from the insidious influence of the thing outside the hull. But some was real and basic. It's one thing to be cursed with carrying another man around in your head—another living, thinking, reasoning being—but it's quite another to share your being with a corpse—to have your brain echoing the disorganization and fragmentation of a dead mind. It brings something of the process of death into you. It's a taint . . . something filthy.

I wouldn't have wished him dead, for all that I hated him. I didn't want his help or his advice or his company or his love. None of them. I would far rather have had clear title to my soul. But alive he was at least knowable. Dead he was something from outside, something alien.

In the end, I woke from that first sleep. One always does. The shadows fled into the crevices where they hide from the light of reason. They always do.

Before we all went to work again, under Nick's direction, I felt that I had to give them all some kind of hope, some motive force that would make them work. I didn't know quite how to do it. Sleep had brought me no nearer to the solution of the problem. But it didn't take much waking thought to arrive at the conclusion that there was only one way—only one possible way—that gave us a snowball's chance in hell of getting out of the lens.

When we were gathered together, ready for the big announcement, Nick was quick to volunteer to take over the engine. He, at least, still fancied himself as something of a hero. Some people aren't changed by anything.

I overruled him.

"If it was the best chance," I said, "then I'd let you take it. If I thought Miss Vogan had any better chance, then she could take it. But I can't trust either of you to do what needs to be done. I can't trust Sam either. By elimination, that leaves one and one only.

"I'll do it myself."

XX

It was seventeen years since I'd last ridden a ship from the bottom end rather than the top, and even then it hadn't exactly been a vocation. It was just something that was occasionally convenient to do and know about. Herault and I used to get about a bit in the days before I took to dreaming and met up with Lapthorn. But riding an engine is something you don't forget. It's like riding a bike. Once you've learned it, you've taken to it.

The *Hooded Swan* was no broken-down ramrod, mind—and she had her unique features, but Sam had taken to her like a duck to water and I figured that I could get by. Only just, maybe, but who else could do even that much?

But it wasn't really me that they were betting on. It was Eve. I had to back my ideas about what was wrong with Eve and how it could be put right. I was the only one who could take Sam's place, and—equally—she was the only one who could take mine. To do that, she had to be brought back from whatever limbo she had retired to.

She had gone out with the *Sister Swan* when it blew. They had blown together. I could think of only one thing that might bring Eve back to life and that was to lock her in a cradle and bring the ship to life around her. If she was going to come back at all she would come back into the ship, enter into ship-consciousness. I had to believe and trust that if we set her up and started a countdown, when the number reached zero she'd be ready and able to do what was needed.

Maybe it was a long shot. Maybe Titus Charlot would have read the whole thing differently and put his own trust in another solution. But as a pilot, I looked at things from the pilot's angle, and despite the fact that I didn't have a great deal of respect for Eve's training or her abilities, I

credited her with a pilot's feeling and a pilot's potential. I
thought she could come through, if things were right for
her. I hoped she would come through, for her own sake,
and for all our sakes. If this play failed we probably
wouldn't get a chance to try any of the alternatives.

I placed Eve in the cradle myself. I hooked up her contacts with the utmost care, and I placed the hood. I made
sure every electrode was clean, and I tried to minimize the
discomfort which would inevitably arise because her head
wasn't the same size and shape as mine.

After that, I reprogrammed the computer to carry us
through the course by which we'd arrived at our present
position. By the time I was through Nick was well advanced
with his resurrection of the nerve-net. I put Sam and Mina
down below in order to do a complete systems check of all
in-ship power systems. As Nick gave us back the sensory
hookups one by one I tested them.

Throughout the whole procedure, Eve never moved a
muscle. But we were only making the ship twitch—we
hadn't got anywhere near bringing her back to life.

Ultimately, we were set to go—or to try. I stationed Nick
to look after Eve and Mina to look after Nick. I kept Sam
down below, in case I needed moral support, inspiration, or
advice.

Before I went below, Nick looked at me with an air of
accusation.

"You better be right," he said.

"You better hope I am," I told him, putting the screws
on a bit because I didn't like his tone of voice. "Let's all add
amen to that. Because I'm going down to start the countdown, and if she isn't awake and active when the countdown closes we may not know a lot about it. If I let the
cannons go without a brain up top and a pair of hands to
help me juggle the power, we could vanish in a puff of blue
smoke. You won't get the chance to say I told you so, unless we happen to meet up in the hereafter."

Nick looked at Eve, absolutely motionless in the cradle,
limp as a rag doll, and I could tell that he was doing most
of his suffering on her behalf.

"Save it," I advised.

"You really think it will work, don't you?" he said.

"What am I, a lunatic?" I said scathingly.

"How do I know?" he retorted.

"If it works," I told him, "then I wasn't."

"How could it fail?" he said. I got the distinct impression that he lacked faith. I couldn't help that. Just as long as he did what he was told he was welcome to do without. I left him to his mental torture, without much sympathy.

I was not really cut out to be an engineer. It was all foreign to my nature and foreign to my touch. I strapped myself in and rediscovered the fact that there's all the difference in the world between a pilot's cradle and an engineer's harness. For one thing, an engine is *big*. The parts of the drive-unit towered above me and crowded around me, and I felt very small hanging in my little alcove. An engineer can't sit down—he needs his freedom of movement. He can do his job with one hand tied behind his back, but he still needs the reach. The instruments are strung out—there's no hood to give direct sensory access to the information. You can't read every dial simultaneously—you have to play partly by ear, partly by feel, and partly by inspired guesswork.

I wasn't happy, but I was comfortable. I knew what I was doing, and I knew that I knew. But I was still scared, still apprehensive. I was very glad that no one was going to get the chance to tell me they told me so, if it didn't work, because I was just in the mood to be sensitive about that kind of thing.

I even had one angle that Sam didn't have, and that was the knowledge of what it felt like from on top. That would be a help, I was sure. The worm always stands to profit from the bird's-eye view. I told myself that, and tried to persuade myself I had a ticket home and not a one-way to hell.

Nick and I called off the routines of the last pre-flight check like a pair of automatons. There was nothing to it. I didn't know how much of a job Nick had done with the sensors, and I didn't really want to know. It had to be good enough, and that was all there was to it. All the superficial checks were fine.

When we finished, I said, "Any sign of life?"

He said, "No."

"OK," I said, "I'm putting her on to warm. Keep your eyes on the panel. Anything flickers that shouldn't flicker, shout."

I hesitated just a fraction of a second, flexing my fingers;

then I began to close the switches and activate the reaction mass. I felt the huge steel case come alive as the motor began to hum inside. Sam was right behind me, strapped in the reserve position. He didn't say a word. I watched the needle climbing as the rhythm of the discharge gathered and increased.

"I'm staying sub-threshold," I said to Nick. "This is just to tickle her up a bit, get the blood flowing. Is anything happening?"

"No."

"Right. Mina, give her a shot." She was standing by with a big stim-shot, supposedly big enough to make the proverbial dead sit up and shout "Geronimo." I gave her time to comply with the instruction.

A faint "OK" came floating back down the circuit. I checked all my dials with religious overcaution. I was still holding steady, sub-threshold, purring along all nice and easy. I counted to fifty in my mind, giving Eve some time, while I set up the elevation sequence; then I began to push up the potential in the chamber—not too quickly and not too far. I let it back down again without developing any thrust.

"Everything holding?" I asked.

"Sound as a bell inside," said Nick, "but *she's* not moving."

"Take her hands," I said, "and put them on the levers. Clasp them and hold them there. See if they'll stay."

Moments later: "I think they'll drop off if I let them go."

"Don't," I said. "Get Mina to take over. Hold them there and keep the grip tight. Nick, keep watching the panel. I'm going to give her another gentle swell."

I let more time pass, giving the drug every chance. I knew it wouldn't work on its own—what was wrong with Eve wasn't a matter of metabolism—but I hoped the swell in the chamber might just push her out and let us know we were on to a good thing.

It didn't.

I won't say I wasn't downhearted, but I'd always known that it would almost certainly go to the acid test.

"She's not responding," said Nick. I could hear Mina's voice in the background, saying something anxiously, but I couldn't catch the words.

"All right," I said. "Eggs in the basket. I'm activating the flux field." The web appeared on the screen in front of me in schematic analogue. There seemed to be more of it than I'd been expecting. It was like some kind of weird flower drawn in colored light.

I eased back on the main control and let some of the power run into the deration field.

"I'm beginning countdown at two-fifty," I said calmly. "Keep her hands on the levers. Activate the program in the computer when I come to a hundred. I've set it to make the first turning maneuver on automatic at dead slow. It's only spinning the ship, but it involves some movement of the levers. Leave the manual override closed. When she feels the levers moving she may come back. If she waits for the cannons to burn she may be late to get into the act but there'll still be a chance. Don't anybody panic—not at any stage. Hold your breath, but *don't let go*. If you get to exhale we'll probably live to tell the tale. Ready?"

"Any time," said Nick.

"Two hundred fifty," I said. "Two hundred forty-nine . . . "

I knew that the numbers would be bouncing around in Eve's head, fed in through the hood. Even the numbers might work the trick. They were steady, and familiar, and she might just find her mind and body falling into step with them.

As the count descended I kept everything steady. It was all easy so far. I had the balance right in my palm. No trouble. I watched the web like a hawk, moving my fingers easily from key to key on the fluction board, getting the feel of the surfaces. I let the thrust build slowly toward the threshold, swelling it insistently, throwing some real power into the nerve-net.

When I reached a hundred it began. It was nothing but a redistribution—only auxiliary power was invoked. This was a maneuver that an ordinary ship couldn't carry out—it wouldn't have the bird's joints or musculature. A conventional ship has to go forward to turn. We didn't. We didn't need to use the cannons.

The control levers were moving now, in Eve's hands. If only Eve's hands would begin to fall in with the movement, to grip of her own accord. . . .

" . . . Eighty-five . . . " I called. " . . . Eighty-four . . . "

Something strangled came over the call-circuit. Something not meant for me. No words, just an expression of some inner tension that had to come out.

"Watch that whine," said Sam, using his ears for me. "Taper off the swell."

I held the growth of the field for a moment, drawing power into the auxiliaries. The correction was only slight. There was plenty of time. No sweat yet.

"Seventy . . . sixty-nine . . . "

"It's not working," said Nick, with a deathly calmness in his voice. He wasn't talking to me, only letting it out. He was tied up as tight as could be. I ignored him.

" . . . Fifty-six . . . fifty-five . . . "

Let go her hands, I wanted to say. Let them go and let them stay on the levers. Trust to her. I couldn't interrupt the count, and it was the last thing I ought to say if I could, but the words echoed in my skull anyway. I was getting ahead of myself. The tension was reaching me. I wanted Eve to wake up before zero. Desperately.

"Mina," said Nick, "you can ease your hands away. I think they'll stay now."

I only wished that I could *see*.

"Twenty-nine . . . twenty-eight . . . "

"I can't," I heard Mina say. "I just can't."

"It doesn't matter," said Nick. "I think it's all right."

" . . . Eighteen . . . seventeen . . . "

I imagined Mina, no tears on her face but eyes afire, her hands white and tight as they clutched Eve's fingers to the controls, unable to let go. Petrified.

"It's all right," whispered Nick—and this time I think he was talking to all of us. "It's all right."

" . . . Five . . . " I said. "Four . . . three . . . two . . . one . . . "

I let go all the impulse from the discharge points as I tongued an inaudible "zero . . . "

. . . And it was picked up.

Eve was with me. The power flooded the deration system, setting the cycle and building the syndromatic reaction. The cannons let go and the MR caught up all the thrust from the cannons like a greedy predator. Sucking all the power into her heart and her guts, the bird flew.

The course we had . . . it was in the computer. The flight-plan we also had. It was only a matter of holding tight, of preserving that most precious balance.

The voice came back down the circuit.

"Steady, Rothgar," she said.

I didn't say a word. It wasn't the time to be shattering anyone's illusions.

I heard Nick's voice, too. "Take us out," he was saying, in a voice which suggested prayer rather than command. "Take us home."

"Yes, captain," she said. Or something like that. I don't know. I don't remember. I only had eyes for the web, and my fingers were dancing on the keys, balancing and feeding, correcting every random break and leak, keeping the whole of the vast field smooth, wrapping the ship up into a neat little parcel, taking her up toward the barrier we would never quite reach.

We played it back exactly as we'd come in. There was no tachyonic hurdle to leap, no phase-flicker to play off. It was easier, so much easier, as though it were all downhill instead of up. A climb and a surge, a leap through the scissure in space, *out* into the known, beautiful, *empty* universe.

We stretched our wings and we soared.

Our hearts swelled, our blood hummed in our veins. We reached out and it was all in our hands, all held, all steady.

And we were through.

Hurtling through vacuous space, decelerating smoothly, releasing the load, and relaxing in our course. Eve overrode the program, realizing that it was all over before she even realized what it was.

I held it, feeling like a juggler performing a difficult trick for the one and only time.

"Did you hear it, Sam?" I said.

"I heard it," he assured me.

"Eve," I said. "Are you listening? You hear me? This is Grainger, Eve. You made it."

When she spoke my name it sounded like the hiss of an angry cat. It was only shock—maybe a touch of horror. She was still slowing the ship, letting her go into a drift. Her moment was over. She was falling back, now, giving way. It didn't matter.

"Take it easy," I said. "It's all over. Damn the rest. They can come and get us. Take us home on stretchers. I don't care. We did our bit. It's all over."

All we had to do was wait.

XXI

———◆———

We were all too tired to have much of a party while we were waiting to be found, but we tried. A good deal of time went by before they got a ship to us, but we didn't discover the reason until they actually reached us. We didn't do any more talking than was necessary through the call-circuit.

Abram Adams came out himself, with a number of his staff, on a small ship called the *Gipsy Rose* which hadn't been on Darlow when we lifted.

It was not until Adams came aboard the *Swan* that we found out how long we had been away. More than a hundred days had passed—in the real world—since the *Swan* had entered the lens. They'd given us up for good and all.

It wasn't only time that had passed on, either. Titus Charlot was dead. He had died believing that he had made a grave and terrible mistake. He gave up the crew of the *Sister Swan* for dead, and he assumed that I had suffered a like fate. I think Adams might have blamed me for causing the old man's death, or at least hastening it, had it not been for the fact that Charlot had been ready and willing to overlook the fact that I'd left him behind. Much later, when I got to thinking about it, I concluded that a trip into the Nightingale was probably the last thing Titus Charlot had *wanted* to do. He was so determined to come because he considered himself to be under an obligation. I'd let him off the hook by stealing the mission. There were no charges waiting to face me when I got back. In fact, quite the reverse. Charlot had taken steps to have it recorded that I— that each and every one of us—had died a hero.

I think my obituary was the nicest thing I ever read.

They'd put Titus Charlot's body in a deep-freeze and sent it home to be buried under the sweet cosmetic surface of his home world. The realization that I was free of him forever came upon me rather slowly. When I first heard the news, I wasn't exactly heartbroken, and my first thought was that it would be nice to be able to scrawl graffiti on his tombstone. But the attitude didn't last. After a while, I was almost sorry to think that I'd left him behind to die with the bitterness of his failure, because—in a way—he hadn't failed. I think he ought to have been allowed to know that. One life lost, and a pair of eyes, but maybe those weren't wholly down to him.

The ship was still New Alexandrian, but I gathered from Zimmer that there was no one quite ready to step into Charlot's shoes yet. I had time in hand, and the chance of a voice in my own future.

Sam stayed with the ship. I didn't want to let him go to wherever old spacemen go when they don't die. Mina stayed too, and with Johnny that would have made a full crew in numerical terms, but numerical terms weren't the only ones to be considered. I didn't really know whether Nick and Eve would want to sign on with me, and I didn't know any way of asking them that wouldn't sound absurd. But they solved the problem for me. They asked me. They had no intention of letting go.

We were becalmed on Darlow for quite some time. The ship was only just about spaceworthy and the crew most certainly was not. It was some days after we limped home that news filtered back through channels to New Alex, and it was several days more before the reaction was felt. Johnny shipped himself back to us at the earliest possible opportunity. I wasn't looking forward to facing him, because I knew that whether Charlot had forgiven me or not, *he* never would. The fact that as things turned out we'd found a moment when we needed him badly, and he hadn't been there to fill the need, only added fuel to the fires of his resentment.

"I just don't understand," he said to me, once he had me cornered. "I know you didn't want Charlot. I see that. But why me? You knew damn well I wanted to go—*needed* to go. *Why?*"

"You wanted your share of the glory?" I said.

"Not that," he told me. "It's more than that."

I knew it. I accepted it. It meant more to him than the fact that we were labeled heroes. He'd wanted something

else—something more personal. How could I explain to
him why I hadn't let him have it?

"I stole it from you," I told him. "The glory, everything.
I stole it because I thought you'd be better off without it."

"Since when did you decide what's good for me?" he demanded.

A fairer question I never heard. There was no answer to
it.

"I wanted to go," he repeated.

I nodded. "I think that's why I left you. I didn't want to
go. Not at all."

"You didn't trust me?" he said.

"No," I admitted.

He waited for me to amplify that, and I tried to carry
on. I owed him some sort of explanation. "You reminded
me of someone," I told him. "Someone I used to know. It
felt . . . uncomfortable. He died, you see . . . you might
say that I killed him. I didn't think you *ought* to want to go.
Maybe not so much because I didn't trust you, maybe more
because I didn't want *you* to trust *me*. You were putting
too much onto my shoulders, do you see? You were putting
pressure on me that I didn't want to take."

"I was right," he reminded me.

"You were right," I agreed. "For all the wrong reasons."

The catch is, I might have added, that that's the way
things happen. For all the wrong reasons. It's the way the
world goes around.

XXII

In my sleep, he keeps coming back. In fragments.

I sometimes have the illusion that I could stick them together again, if I only knew how.

I have looked out of alien eyes at a certain alien world, perhaps a thousand times. He would not tell me where it is, but I know. In the end, he couldn't stop me knowing. I know where he came from. But I won't be telling Titus Charlot or anyone like him. I won't be inviting anyone to a private nova party. It's not for me to interfere. The universe can go its own way. It's not that I don't want to get involved, it's just that I haven't the qualifications to play the game of God.

I seem to know that world well. I have not seen so much, nor understood so much, of his experiences with other hosts. There is less of such experience left . . . perhaps less of such experience is truly his.

Every now and again, but only when I am asleep, I dream that I might one day go to the world from which he came, and land as the Gallacellan did so many centuries ago. I might land my ship, and open the airlock, and step out to breathe in the air. I might stand with my feet in the grass, and cough politely, and say, "Is anybody there?"

When I dream that way, I always wake sweating. I don't know why I'm so afraid.

Maybe for all the wrong reasons.

Brian Stableford
The Paradise Game 60p

Pharos — a planet that was the incarnation of all that people were conditioned to believe beautiful — its environment unpolluted and perfect, its inhabitants humanoid, gullible and female. Grainger is despatched in the starship *Hooded Swan* to investigate the world of Pharos, only to discover that this Paradise has a serpent of its own . . .

Promised Land 60p

Starship *Zodiac* carried its cargo of men and women across the centuries-wide interstellar gulf between Earth and Chao Phrya and delivered its passengers into a Promised Land. Into this hostile and mysterious world comes Grainger aboard his starship *Hooded Swan* in pursuit of an alien girl who could hold the key to the enigma of Chao Phrya . . .

The Fenris Device 60p

On an inhospitable planet where no man has ventured before lies the wreck of a Gallacellan warship — the vehicle of the oldest spacefaring race in the galaxy. Aboard the wreck is a legendary weapon — The Fenris Device . . . a legend strong enough to attract the masters of the *Hooded Swan* in their thirst for knowledge.

Bob Shaw
A Wreath of Stars 60p

Thornton's Planet is an anti-neutrino planet whose appearance causes a wave of panic . . . then comes news from the African state of Barandi; miners wearing magniluct lenses have seen ghosts in the mine passages . . . the passage of Thornton's Planet has had further-reaching effects on Earth than anyone could have imagined . . .

'Shaw is improving with everything he does . . . the most accomplished of the younger British stable' OBSERVER

Bob Shaw
Cosmic Kaleidoscope 70p

From the prize-winning author of *Orbitsville*, nine stories which demonstrate Shaw's superb imaginative range and cynically humorous approach to the world of the future.

Harlan Ellison
Deathbird Stories 80p

'The grimoires and *Necronomicons* of the gods of the freeway, of the ghetto blacks, of the coaxial cable; the paingod and the rock god and the god of neon . . . the gods that live in city streets and slot machines. The God of Smog and the God of Freudian Guilt. The Machine God. Know them now . . . they rule the nights through which we move'
HARLAN ELLISON

Richard Cowper
The Custodians 60p

'The Custodians': A room constructed at the intersection of mysterious force fields, so that anyone entering can foresee the future . . . 'Paradise Beach': A wall-screen that attunes itself to the individual perceptions of the onlooker . . . 'Piper at the Gates of Dawn': The magical tale of an old storyteller, an enchanted piper and a mysterious white bird . . .'

You can buy these and other Pan Books from booksellers and newsagents; or direct from the following address:
Pan Books, Sales Office, Cavaye Place, London SW10 9PG
Send purchase price plus 20p for the first book and 10p for each additional book, to allow for postage and packing
Prices quoted are applicable in the UK

While every effort is made to keep prices low, it is sometimes necessary to increase prices at short notice. Pan Books reserve the right to show on covers and charge new retail prices which may differ from those advertised in the text or elsewhere